NETSUKE

Netsuke

A NOVEL

Rikki Ducornet

COFFEE HOUSE PRESS :: MINNEAPOLIS :: 2011

Coffee House Press books are available to the trade through our primary distributor, Consortium Book Sales & Distribution, www.cbsd.com or (800) 283-3572. For personal orders, catalogs, or other information, write to: info@coffeehousepress.org.

Coffee House Press is a nonprofit literary publishing house. Support from private foundations, corporate giving programs, government programs, and generous individuals helps make the publication of our books possible. We gratefully acknowledge their support in detail in the back of this book.

To you and our many readers around the world,
we send our thanks for your continuing support.

LIBRARY OF CONGRESS CIP INFORMATION

Ducornet, Rikki, 1943–

Netsuke : a novel / by Rikki Ducornet.

p. cm.

ISBN 978-1-56689-253-7 (alk. paper)

I. Title.

PS3554.U279N48 2011

813'.54—DC22

2010038004

PRINTED IN CANADA

1 3 5 7 9 8 6 4 2

FIRST EDITION | FIRST PRINTING

NETSUKE

I am my own hiding place.
—JOË BOUSQUET

One

Although it is still very early, the wealth of the day is upon him.

He is running. He is listening to Monteverde and he is running. He is very muscled and lean. He lopes along hungry as a wolf. There is something regal about the canopy of leaves above him. The sun has only just lifted over the rim of the world.

His days are made up of what he calls "real time" and "the interstices." Real time provides an identity, a footing. The interstices, however, provide him with a life. The sun begins to spill onto the path. He runs dappled with light. Hooked to Monteverde, he doesn't hear the birds rioting in the trees. He runs like a creature of the woods before the world truly began. Long before the first great cities of the world had ever been conceived. He is aware of his sex when he runs.

There is a pretty woman, surely half his age, running toward him. As they are about to pass one another, his eyes leap into hers. She slows down and turning, runs backwards, looking at him. When he glances over his shoulder, she bursts into laughter. A gentle breeze lifts. The day shimmers with the music of Monteverde. Still laughing, she turns away and runs into the trees. It is like a movie, maybe an animated cartoon: he playing the centaur to her nymph. Yes, that's it: a centaur.

In an instant the world compresses into one point of heat and light. Off the path now, deep in the trees, they begin to devour one another's tongue and teeth, panting each time they surface for air. He pushes her up against a tree and takes her. She burns at the center of his life. He will never weary of fucking her. She rides him, he rides her; she drowns, he swims into her depths; she cries out; she trembles; she says wow and laughs again, but very quietly; he emerges from her, and with a graceful, almost imperceptible gesture, rearranges his cock; he hesitates a moment; he tenderly brushes her cheek with the back of his hand and says:

"Sorry, Sweetheart. I've got to go to work."

"Yeah." She nods, and beams down at him as he fumbles with the lace of his sneaker. She sighs; she, too, pulls herself together. "So what's work?" she asks, lightly. Not wanting to appear overly curious. Needful.

"Psychoanalysis," he says, eager now to get on his way. He thinks she looks like a kid, her straw-colored hair barely holding in a rubber band. A sweet-looking kid. A daisy, among many of the field.

"Bye, Sweetheart," he says, and off he goes, turning once to smile at her and wave, the gesture charming, attentive, and yet . . .

"Hey!" she calls out after him. He is vanishing down the path. "Hey!"

⁓

Theirs is a big city.

Back home he showers and works up a lather. He's Neptune in a sea of foam. He is a god leaping from the interstices back to the real world. He recalls that for the gods, the real world was, in fact, the interstices: a playground, a mirror of the heavens, a theater. Each morning after his run is like this: he, in a lather, reflecting, pummeled by water. He will stay in the shower for an hour, making himself over, making himself new. The process, he thinks, is alchemical. Today he is feeling especially philosophical. He considers the nature of women. The daisies of the field, so fuckable, so breakable. The ones who call out Hey! and stamp their feet in irritation, like mares. The ones who blossom early, only to succumb to nerves. Those who startle easily and sour in an instant; love with them is like sucking lemons. The lazy, careless women in need of pedicures, who, when darkness falls, can be seen lolling about, unkempt, in tapas bars. The aging actresses, their sweet vulnerabilities on parade. Incandescent alcoholics as troublesome as fever dreams, fantastic in the *early hours of the evening, but only then. The chameleons. The gorgeous exotics prone to outbursts of temper. The luscious North Africans, their balaclava pussies. The antelope who cannot settle down—a good fuck on an airplane, taxicab, the train. The new mistress one fucks before sitting down to dinner with one's wife. The women who give courage (these are rare). The wild ones with magenta manes who wear boots in all seasons. The whore who brought down Enkidu,* who showed him the things a woman knows how to do. *The tribal types who like sex in clusters. The women who, at Christmas, consider suicide. The frisky ones. The ones who talk too much. The ones who kill with silence. The risk takers. The ones with Big Ideas. The death cunts who kill with a look. The tender ones, the Feyaways, like islands, who love in cautious isolation, who rub one's feet; they have juicers. One abandons them judiciously, all the while cooing like a dove. The clients whom one fucks in the name of a Unique Experiment. The wives whom one betrays, extravagantly. The current wife: Akiko. The one for whom the interstices were superseded, if only briefly, by the Real. Akiko. Whose beauty no longer troubles his sleep. (His world is mazed with cunts and he has not yearned for hers in centuries.)*

An old Prince of Darkness—this is what he has become. *His teeth worn to the gums, his tongue swollen with overuse, his cock, like his heart, close to breaking.*

1

A SMALL PRIVATE PARK that Akiko has transformed into a scene from *The Tale of Genji* extends beyond the house; it has a broad path that leads to the public trails, thickets, a wetland, a lake.

I run from our house into the public land in the mornings, often alone, in the early light. I can run for over an hour without hearing the hum of city traffic. This early in the day, there is something more than royal about this domain: it is mythical. I run toward the past—not my own past, mind you, but a distant, primal past. A past in which my own infancy, or the current lousy state of affairs, or even the great city beyond the bluff—is unimaginable.

Today when I return to the house, I see the lights are on in Akiko's studio. This means I will find a thermos of fresh green tea waiting for me on the kitchen counter. A sweet gesture, considering how evasive I am with her. Akiko has come to confuse my evasiveness with a retiring nature. In her words, I am "the silent type." My silence conceals a wealth of worlds best left undisclosed.

We have been together ten years. Long enough for my idiosyncrasies to have faded into invisibility. Akiko, too, has faded. She is the white noise I have come to depend upon and possibly cannot live without. Akiko is witchy, clairvoyant. Her astonishing dreams are astute, surgical. They keep me on my toes. This marriage of ours puts us both at risk. She is in danger because I lie incessantly and the habit of these lies has blunted her gift and confused her. Love has caused her to distrust her own intuitions. Yet I am in danger also, because I cannot help but offer her clues. It is inevitable that sooner or later I will falter, offer one clue too many and in this way bring us both down. When I fall, she will fall with me. Perhaps this is a comfort of a kind.

2

My Practice belongs to a shelf in the Devil's Kitchen. Insulated, above suspicion, I take my pleasure and am sustained by the sorrow of others. Their carnality. The ceaseless ebb and tide of human inconstancy, negligence, cowardice.

In the world I know, everyone is betrayed sooner or later.

The Practice is not of my own making. I mean: it is an inheritance of a kind. I have wandered its maze since infancy. I do not know another way to live. I often wish I did. The Practice is the inevitable extension of my own private dilemma. It is lethal, and yet without it I would perish. Assiduously, I portion out its poisons. Assiduously, I orchestrate the days. Like a game of chess, the Practice proposes an infinite set of circumstances. Or, rather, not exactly infinite. For I begin to—and this admission is terrifying—to see how redundant, how *compressed,* the games are.

My clients are thwarted, famished, and lonely. Inevitably, sooner or later, I seize upon and penetrate the one who has wanted this from me from the first instant. Or has taken time but has come around to wanting it. For a client, fucking the doctor is always perceived as a triumph. Although I am always curious from the start. In this way

I am made. If the client is attractive I cannot help but wonder: is she/he fuckable? An outrageous determination. And yet: fucking is the one determinism. The one inevitability. In this way it is exactly like death. You know you'll fuck, be fucked; you know you'll die and maybe be murdered. And maybe murder.

I've known transcendent sex, but its promise frightens me. The risks of delight are immense. The infant feeding at the madwoman's breast, slipping deliciously in and out of slumber, is fiercely smacked. Smacked when he sups, he is quickly weaned. In no time he has learned to suck up, bite, and wean. Always watchful for the hook, he travels deep into the world of men with his deft set of sharpened tools. He will become a hoodlum, a maniac, a soldier; he will become a priest, a prison guard, a cop. A dogmatist, a patriarch—decidedly a public danger. He will become a psychoanalyst. He will have a Practice.

He will learn to dissemble. He will laugh like a wolf. He will cut through the city streets like a blade through water. His realm will be the streets, their secret stores of pleasure, their secret doors (I have a drawer full of keys!) opening to wondrous rooms, unfamiliar rooms, shabby rooms. He is attracted to, appalled by, shabby rooms. The street boy's spare depot, the shopgirl's cluttered cheese box, the saturated confusion of the drag queen's aviary, her floor slick with hairspray and powder. (He must take care to shed these scents, to kick the dust up behind him before returning home.)

Unlike a female client, a man in a wig, a boy smelling of malnutrition, are not likely to hire a lawyer.

In recent years I have pretty much neglected Akiko. These days we live in something of a parallel universe. Sometimes I catch a glimpse of her strolling the garden in her dreamy way. Sometimes she vanishes for a week or more. My wife displays her work in distant cities where it is apparently much appreciated. As it should be.

There are times when I admire her imagination. The autonomy it assures her (and I so needful of company!). Day after day she paces her studio with her scissors, the glue pot, those images she has culled from all times and places. She's like a creature from a fairy tale, my Akiko: beautiful, ethereal, living much of her life alone with her scissors and, in silence, piecing scraps of paper together.

Always she returns from her journeys with stories and presents for me. Rare netsuke, for example, although I have so little interest in aesthetic devices.

3

I LEAVE CLUES BEHIND both purposefully and inadvertently. Inadvertently because I do not wish to be discovered; I do not wish to hurt Akiko. There is a self within me who longs, at least from time to time, if more and more sporadically, to live a simple, tender life. Or, if this is beyond my powers, to engage the interstices with discretion, without harming Akiko. Yes. Without bringing her to harm.

Purposefully because I long to be discovered as I always have, since infancy, to receive the punishment that is my due. To risk annihilation. I court annihilation.

Deception is tiresome. It begins to seriously leech my resources, my strength, my powers of intellect, my time. And because there is a self within me who would crush Akiko's gentle neck. Who knows? Perhaps one day we will die together in a conflagration. Our own conflagration in a world that everywhere is burning.

Recently I made trouble for myself with a shopgirl. Such women are shameless; they are under the erroneous impression that other women, women like Akiko, are not. One will not disabuse them.

She could be my daughter, this overheated wench worthy of Wycherley. (She'd play Lucy, the buxom lady's maid.) Neurotic, cummy, self-aggrandizing, a braggart. I should know better. The new girl Friday to my wife's framer. My clairvoyant Akiko hated her on sight, whereas I couldn't take my eyes off her. We eye fucked straight away. The transaction ended badly, with Lucy spilling coffee on Akiko's portfolio. For this she was fired, if only briefly. Later in the week she called my office and begged me to intercede in her favor. As Akiko—in an unprecedented temper—had taken her business elsewhere and so could not know, I did as I was asked. Lucy triumphant, therefore, a thing I could not help but profit from. Her little deed amused the cad that dwells within. It should have ended after an afternoon's burn between two evildoers, but I was hooked. Encounters such as this enliven the days. And so the thing persisted.

Lucy was like a spoiled child; we played hard together. She teased me, she needled, she longed to see our house, Akiko's and mine. She hungered like a little cat for a taste of the fish set out upon the master's table. And so as soon as Akiko was away—clear across the country—the cats did counterfeit domestic bliss. (I should add that, if Lucy's transparency amused me, her needling also hardened me against her. Within the interstices, her place would always be secondary.) I knew our setup would floor her. She would be envious; she was. When I saw the green cinders leaping from those malicious eyes, I feared I had, once again, gone too far. (As when fucking the little blonde who does our taxes.)

We tumbled around the house like pandas. I spun her like a top. I rolled her about this way and that. We managed to despoil every room and knock over a small red lacquer box, although the house is sparely decorated. I knew enough to keep her out of the studio, but when she saw a large collage suspended above our bed, she raged: *The bitch doesn't deserve all this!* At that instant I could see her a decade down the road: flushed, fighting fat, bitter.

She needed soothing. I made her a kir, got out the snacks, and then, at night's fall, took her to the marriage bed.

Lucy was mollified by this ultimate betrayal; like Scrooge McDuck, a rainbow, a pot of gold spun above her head. I let her dream although I planned to dump her; she was—I could see it—pretty crazy, possibly borderline psychotic. I feared—and rightly so—an unregulated nature. It would be a job to manage the affair. I began to worm my way out of it.

As we cuddled and whispered together into the night, I revealed my sorry life; the doctor's life is not his own. Clients all in danger of collapse—or worse—from one moment to the next. The midnight calls from the hospital, fire department, or police. I made it clear our time together was possible only because of an unusual synchronicity: Akiko's opening in New York and the departure of a client, recently terminated and who had left for Australia where he intended to start up his own practice devoted to a thing he knew from the inside out: the misuse of infants and children by those who are depended upon for protection.

Lucy began to weep, poor, winsome brat! In her early teens an uncle had been inappropriate. I told her she was fortunate it had not happened sooner.

"Not sooner!" she surfaced like a porpoise from the foamy sheets. "So *later* is O.K.? Fuck that! Fuck you! I can't believe you said that!"

Yet when I made to lick her tits she sighed and yawned, needful of a pre-dawn nap. (It is she who broke the shell; I am sure of it!)

—————

The minute Akiko returned, she knew something was amiss. She barely touched the take-out sushi, artfully presented, but roamed the house mumbling that it *looked odd,* it *felt odd*. She wondered if it had actually shifted, if ever so slightly, on its foundations. Had there been a small earthquake? A torrential rain? And then she found the shell. A precious shell from Indonesia, spotted and pronged; a thing I'd never paid any attention to. It was a rarity, and now it was broken.

For a time Akiko wore an irritated look; a furrow appeared on her lovely forehead. I must admit it turned me on. The oddest things do.

4

THE PRACTICE IS CONTAINED within two home cabinets situated at the entrance to our property, but my clients do not know there is a house beyond, nestled in the woods; Akiko's studio, as well, is invisible. Perched upon the edge of a small ravine, both appear to soar above the canopy. From within our rooms, Akiko notices and points out to me the deer, the snowy owls, and seasonal hummingbirds.

The home cabinets are well rooted to the ground by a stone path and garden, all of Akiko's design. My wife is addicted to perfection and adheres to a dogmatic system both ancient and alien to me. And beneficial. In terms of my need to dissemble, she is my greatest gift. The cabinets are impeccably set out. They are spare and they are superb. Each has its own waiting room. The cabinets both open to a hallway that leads to my own private library and office.

One of the cabinets I call Spells. I cannot enter it without my heart beating faster. The other I call Drear. If Spells is devoted to the pleasures of transgression, Drear belongs to all the rest: Lutherans, a defrocked priest, a wafer-thin old maid, a psychopath who has bungled more surgeries than he has toes, the retired night watchman who squanders his pension on whores and whose wife of forty years is suing for divorce. There is also the CEO of a local company undoubtedly responsible for my city's dramatic number of birth defects, a college professor—the most tedious of the bunch—who drones on and on about a lost inheritance and his wife's dismal affair with the family dentist. (There was once a young scholar I took a fatherly interest in and who managed to elicit real tenderness.) (Do not think me incapable of tenderness.)

Sometimes a client will move up from Drear to Spells, even after many years. There was an actress once, as rageful as a bloody axe, who over time was soothed and then began—it seemed miraculous—to flourish. One day I saw how beautiful she had become, how vigorous, how eager for the world and its delights; how desirous, also, of transgression.

I invented an excuse, claimed Drear needed to be reconfigured, and moved her to Spells. There I allowed her to seduce me: "I always," she told me on her knees, "wanted this." The affair triggered a shift in her expectations and charisma; she landed a major role downtown. That was ten years ago. And if her roles are now less glamorous, she still invites me to opening nights.

Spells is the theater where my clients and I break all the rules. And this under the banner of Mindful Subversion, Convulsive Beauty. What happens here is stunning, somehow always unique, if orchestrated. I never forget that I am dealing with people who, despite their determinisms, their needful tenderness, their pride, can at any moment decide to kill me or call their lawyers. And so Spells is oiled with solicitude and sweetness and the infinite capacity that seems to be mine to convey that each transgression is unprecedented.

To assure this impression, I have at times and after a period of months or weeks, revealed a previous violation many, many years before when I was green and still vulnerable. Such a revelation convinces the most skeptical of my good intentions, my passionate interest in them, and the anomaly our love affair represents. The lady in question, now a mistress, will assure me that my secret is safe with her, as safe as she believes she is with me. The affair remains circumscribed within the process of recovery.

I do not accept gifts—apart from the little love gifts, so like those of high school girls, I simply cannot refuse. I explain that because our lovemaking is an extension of our work together, the fee will be the same. In this way I become my client's whore. Yet I always manage to act professionally. My infatuations are in the service of knowledge. My clients love this! We fuck in the stellar radiance of knowledge and love. I am enamored of my profession.

The women are intelligent, sexy, neurotic, funny, inventive, feisty, sprightly, and they are in need of me. They do yoga, tai chi; they are in fine fettle and in great shape. They play tennis; they go to the sporting club. They get massages and go to botox parties. They are as sleek as seals.

The men . . . this is more complicated.

5

Back to Akiko.

⁓

My wife sells her curious work for astonishing amounts of money and so receives the bounty of my friendship without ambiguity. I do not "support" her and yet I do provide security, a sense of belonging, of having a place in the world. We are, after all, a couple. It never occurs to her that, as she cooks glue in her bower, I am extending the meaning, the expectations, the boundaries, and even the vocabulary of the therapeutic relationship. At the end of a long day, as I enjoy the raw oysters she has provided for my benefit, the Fanny Bays I especially appreciate, I think, I always do: *Why tell her? Why torment her?*

And yet there are those times I would grab her by the hair and spit it all up in her face. Her pleasure in our life sending me into a rage difficult to contain. In these moments I must drop a clue or else explode.

I tell her about a female patient's sexual interest in dangerous men; a beautiful woman, milky skin; a strawberry blonde. I watch for signs. My wife puts down her fork and grows very still.

I tell her about my concern for this patient's safety. I see Akiko's nostrils flare. My wife is gentle, rational. Coolly she says, well, of course you are concerned. This is what your work is all about. Your deep concern. For other people.

"But this is different," I tell her. "She puts herself directly in harm's way. She has never known anything but rough sex. She fucks in toilets. She's this beautiful woman and gives blowjobs—"

"Stop it!" Akiko hits the table with her fist. "I don't!" she cries out, her white cheeks rouged with dismay, "I don't want to know about patients' sexual lives! And I don't! I don't think you, *goddamnit!* should be telling me this. I'm not supposed to know this!"

I was unexpectedly floored by this outburst, I was shamed. And fearful, also. Dropping clues is always a grave error and so I was quick to soothe her. I agreed that such problems were best kept locked away in Spells.

"Spells?"

"Ah." I felt dizzy, a delicious feeling of descent into a pool of very deep water. A cooling pool. It was risky, another clue inadvertently dropped. But there was the weight, the gravitas of our decade together, Akiko's and mine; I felt safe, and so I said: "Spells. My little name for the sessions. The more difficult sessions."

"Wow," she said, considering. "I didn't know. That's interesting. I'm sorry," she added, coming to me then and putting her arm around me. "After all this time together and still there is so much I don't understand. Your work is *strange!"* she laughed, perhaps benevolently. "But. Understand. It's hard to think about, you know, the women, hour after hour, talking about their sexual lives. I'm not always—how could I be? Up for it. I mean: the knowledge of that."

I thought about what to say next. The best way to diffuse the moment, to erase the clues. An *apology,* I thought. An apology is called for.

"I am sorry," I said to her. "What I did was inconsiderate."

"You're really sweet," she said. "I think we need a break. A little time away together." It was true; we had not been away alone together for well over a year. There was so little time for that, and the risks were enormous.

"As soon as the Practice lightens up a bit," I told her, "we'll go away. We'll go off together." At once I could see I had hit upon exactly the right thing to say: *we'll go off together,* I repeated.

6

AKIKO HAD JUST RECEIVED a very large box of old papers from Bangladesh and Ethiopia, and so would, I knew, be occupied all evening unpacking and sorting these out. There was a time, and it was sweet, it was merry, when she would share these treasures with me and exclaim, with excited chirps, so like a child's, her delight in a particular set of images or an image. Her collages rely on exotic scenes from places far away in space and time, which she deftly manipulates. The finished work is unusually big, the size of doors. She is currently at work on a triptych that, when done, will be over eight feet high and twelve feet across. This work has been commissioned by a museum in Basil? Beirut? No: Berlin.

Perhaps my own notoriety will one day match hers. It is *knowledge* that interests me, although I would never deny the essential nature of art in our lives. Currently, I am writing a book; a large book; I am in the process of ordering several decades of notes and reflections. The tough question is, dare I reveal the nature of my investigations; dare I, finally, openly discuss Spells? And if so, am I "up" for the task of convincing the world that this work of mine is of real value; that it is not perverse; it is not "criminal," but rooted in real tenderness, yes: it is impelled by, informed by, animated by *love*. If the inquiry is unabashedly rooted in the erotic impulse, it is also profoundly—and how could it be otherwise?—*philosophical!* Why shouldn't there be a central place for lust in psychological inquiry?

And if I am called the Marquis de Sade of psychiatry, what of it? Detested by some, venerated by others.

A dangerous business in this proud, prudish land of ours. One risks being confused with horny priests. But, the body *is* imperious. And lust—we *all* know this!—is king! Why separate lust from the equation? As if. As if! An attractive man, a beautiful woman can spend an hour together in the isolation of the therapist's compartment without thinking of cunt and cock! Without wondering what this particular cunt or cock is like! Because there are fascinating variations! Because there is always the promise of some mystery as yet unveiled! That this particular cunt will be dramatically unlike the last!

And yet, simultaneously, there is the reassuring knowledge that a cunt is a cunt is a cunt! One will uncover an old familiar friend! One's cock, one's *heart!* is reassured and grateful. The danger has passed, lust is engaged, one frolics, one rejoices. Yes. That's it: one rejoices!

Or. Or not. One is angry, perhaps. One wanted more. One is wistful. Impatient. One is, I am, more and more often: bored. And she weeps. She blames herself. Her disastrous past. That nasty interlude in infancy with the wayward grandpapa. The violin teacher who poked her indiscreetly. The mother's lover or daddy's best friend. One will do the best one can—one always has to reassure her. And with patience and artful caresses, bring her to the happy land at last. So that she will return to Spells with the little gift one *does* accept: the curious seedpod found in the country road, a paperback on tantric sex, a handful of sand from a beach in Mexico.

"You concern yourself with Heaven," I joked to Akiko the next night over dinner—for her triptych, inspired by Bosch, has a scene of Paradise at its center; referring to my Practice I said: "I concern myself with Hell."

"Then we shall share limbo," she said, I thought mysteriously. "If you give me Heaven and take Hell on alone— that *is* your intention?" she pressed me, I thought somewhat waggishly, "to keep Hell to yourself?"

"All to myself!" I declared and lifted my glass to hers.

But I thought this: Spells is not Hell. Well, sometimes. Not always. My patients thrive, actually. How could it be otherwise? We all love to be desired; fucking makes our day. Sometimes I feel like a tantric temple whore fucking in the name of the gods in a sacred space.

But no. That's not it, either. My patients are too crazy, too edgy, too needy, often *too damned mean* to fit that transcendent mode. They like it down and dirty. They want it hard and bad and so do I. In this way I am like them.

7

A DAY OF CONTRASTS. Akiko, taken up with the garden, plants shrubbery, all Japanese. Firs or pines. (Or both. I do not know anything about plants.) She has a longing for a world she never knew, or rather, has caught mere glimpses of on brief visits to the places of her parent's infancies, having loved, above all, the gardens, simultaneously glamorous and spare. She, too, is glamorous and spare, as is the house, its luminous spaces solarized by things that give off light: lacquer ware, ceramics. (The world *solarized* is hers; a word I had never heard spoken aloud before I met her.) My irritation with marriage suggests that my wife is precious, perhaps. *Snip, snap,* she trims the shrubbery; I see her gaze for hours at a thing to assure some perfection invisible to me. For days she considers a view beyond a reach of trees, beneath a bough, between this sprig and that; she considers her entire universe in the same way she does her collages. When I first met her and I asked her what she did, she said, Oh, I rush after beauty! It's something of a habit, a compulsion— that instant her laughter filled me with joy. And although it had never happened before, our paths began to cross. We met for lunch. She told me about things I had never heard about, let alone thought about. Netsuke.

The frottages of Max Ernst. I began to reconsider the collections of Mexican folk art I had bought hastily, without much thought. I began to disengage from my marriage. I scheduled Akiko in. I began to plan my weeks around her.

Today, as Akiko roams the grounds, I am locked away in Drear with a forlorn house painter, a man both self deprecating and pretentious, who obsesses over bushes of another kind, Kaitlin, a high school sweetheart whose thatch bubbled like a sea anemone in the bath. Black, luxuriant. Where, he wonders (he has for years) is Kaitlin now? She'd be sixty-four, as is he. He envies me (we are roughly the same age) for my full head of hair. Kaitlin must be gray by now. And my salary. Gazing out the picture window at one of Akiko's impeccable vistas, he says: you have more, much more, than I ever even dared *aspire* to.

"I should have *dared!*" he cries out, his voice strangled by a sob, "and now I'm bald and Kaitlin, *all* the Kaitlins, out of reach."

Then he tells me his terrible tale.

Early in the week he had managed to slip away from his wife, who treats him imperiously and with a chronic distrust—for a full two hours. He found what he wanted: a peepshow. (I know the place he means; a dismal joint that needs an airing out, new carpeting, and better bathroom fixtures, etc.) He paid his money, sat down alone in the little cell provided, and waited breathlessly for a glimpse of Kaitlin in the bath, one last glimpse! For this was exactly how he imagined it, that the peepshow would provide a trip back in time. The woman appeared and without ceremony spread her legs, her pussy as hairless as an omelet. The experience has devastated him.

For the rest of the hour, he rambles on and on about Kaitlin, his own wife's ineptitudes, her packaged mashed potatoes, the way everything around him is shutting down, the fact that nothing since that view of Kaitlin in the bathtub has answered his hopes; the terrible memory of seeing a fellow named Brad necking with his sweetheart at the drive-in nearly fifty years ago, how the sorrow of that moment has haunted him throughout his life.

"I cannot shake it, Doctor! I cannot shake it!"

My client's words clatter like gravel on the roof of my mind. I begin to wonder what Akiko has planned for dinner. I think: *pad thai,* attempting telepathy.

———

As important as ideas are, nothing serves the self better than the flesh.

Fucking, at its best, is silent. And yet what I have learned in my Practice is this: people want to talk about it all the time.

———

That evening over Akiko's gorgeous saffroned scallops I blurted:

"An endless day! Endless. Tedious. How good these are!" I told her, feeling unusually expansive. "The hours away from you are long."

"It will be good," said my wife, "when we can finally get away together."

But I cannot take a vacation. For one thing, a vacation means spending hour after hour in close proximity to Akiko and I might drop another clue. I always do. I cannot help myself. Worse than that I might find myself spilling more than clues.

And she is a sweet person; my wife is a beautiful person. Kind. Perhaps too kind. A love like hers demands too much. She has her own practice. She practices innocence, blindness even. And this despite her worldliness, her sophistication.

We were discussing my book.

"All this *talk* I do with them!" I blurted out, impatient all at once with everything, "be damned! Let them go out and burn off their defeats with unbridled promiscuity!"

Akiko took this as a joke of course.

"Might work," she said. "Except sex is pretty much what fucked them up in the first place."

It is possible that, if I have lost patience with ideas and with the vehicle that conveys them from our teeth and tongue and out into the air, it is because so many of my clients don't know how to think. Inevitably they confuse apples with oranges. Because their parents confused love with hate, they have never learned how to listen to the inner logic of the flesh. Their lifesaving *intuitive* capacities must be uncovered, honed, and spurred.

My science is an *embodied* science.

There was a time, not very long ago, a lifetime ago, when he had loved Akiko as he had never loved before, or, at least, this is how it seemed. In Akiko he was sure he had found someone incapable of viciousness, brilliant, worthy. Yet even this was not enough to keep him from the things he is compelled to do to keep his head above water. He wades in heavy, black water that is always threatening to flood his life. There was a time with Akiko when the danger receded, but one day he awakened beside her and the safety she brought him had dissolved. Now he wears his horror in the world like a cloak and only in Spells or at the offset of a liaison can he shake it off.

The proximity of the house he shares with his wife and the room where he betrays her and establishes his illicit itineraries has become problematic. He begins to consider shifting Spells to an office downtown. A downtown office is easy to justify. There are potential clients put off by the drive out to a residential neighborhood: a drive both time-consuming and expensive. He tells Akiko a downtown office will extend his clientele.

The Cutter has much to do with this. She is his current infatuation and perhaps his most dangerous. Lucy is risky, but she is a lightweight. If Akiko found out, she would be angry but not severely undone. He would be forgiven. But the Cutter. She is acute bad weather.

He knows he must manage the affair better than he has; that he will have to end it before long. Weathers of all kinds have begun to change. He begins to seriously resent his wife's purity. And yet he is—although he won't be for long—grateful for her capacity to both love him and give him a great deal of room. He thinks it is fortunate, that she, too, needs room.

For now all the rest is the edge upon which he glides. It is a necessary edge; he would not know how to live without it. But it is growing sharper and soon it will be razor thin. So there is this edge and on either side the dark water that will someday claim him. There is no way out of it. None that he can see.

The downtown cabinet is his way of acknowledging to himself the risk he is in and the essential part risk plays in his life. These days he sleeps little, but when he does it is like sinking in cold mud. He awakens bruised and shaken. At dawn he enters the bathroom to shower. But first he goes to the mirror and examines his teeth.

There is a brief moment when he sees Akiko carrying an armful of pruned branches against her chest. In that moment, there is no understanding why, he is over-whelmed with loss. He wonders if they will survive the winter.

There is a daughter, from a second marriage, he is not allowed to see. He begins to think about her. And then he thinks about other things.

8

THE MODERNIST AESTHETIC PERSISTS; it never loses its power to charm. The new cabinet will be spare, furnished in Eames, black or buff leathers, a Noguchi glass table floating above a large tribal rug, paper lamps that appear to float down from the ceiling and up from the floor.

Akiko is good at transforming neutral rooms into something astonishing. She calls this subversion. Shopping together we look happy. Perhaps we are, acquiring beautiful things. Once the tribal rug—startling in indigo and madder—is rolled up and tagged with our name, we go off to Mr. Taka's shop to acquire a few more netsuke. And a cabinet to keep them, along with the others she has bought me over the years. I approve the extravagance. Netsuke go up in value all the time, and the curiosity cabinet will warm up the room's cool weather.

For now the netsuke are housed in Drear. I tell Akiko how useful they have been in the Practice, stories she has heard before and always likes to hear again. An anorexic client once held up a devil with a protruding belly and said she saw herself. A librarian, the victim of a supernatural tormentor, recognized her dilemma in an ivory clam about to be torn apart by a crab. We traced the crab back to a school principal who liked to paddle unruly girls. As if the paddle were not enough, this monster had a way-ward middle finger.

At Mr. Taka's, we are taken by a small series in the style of Yoshimura Shuzan, who was, Taka tells us, the greatest carver of all time. But the forgeries are excellent and as Mr. Taka passes them to us, Akiko cries out.

"Look how they appear to shriek and howl and even *buzz!*" You will notice a tendency in her to overstate, but Taka agreed; the Shuzans and the best done in his manner are the most expressive in the world.

"I once saw an authentic Shuzan," he tells us. "Although it was displayed along with a number of other exceptional pieces, it called attention to itself, just as you say. It *did* buzz—that's it exactly! Like a hornet in a rage. What is extraordinary," he persists, looking through his books to find us a picture of the piece, "is the amount of manic energy Shuzan can pack into a thing so small and of such humble materials. Here! Look!" Mr. Taka strokes the photograph almost tenderly. "Look at the sensuality of the colors. The reds above all. The passage of time has imparted such luminosity! In another hundred years, in a thousand years, the colors will be even more wonderful!" We watch as this diminutive man, a severely elegant man, slides the book back into its case.

"When lacquer adheres this well to wood," he continues excitedly, "the two cleave together. It is a passionate embrace." He laughs.

I find myself taken by the little things. I realized that I had not paid them enough attention. I liked Mr. Taka, too, this intelligent man who understands passion as well as I. I will repeat what I have heard to the pretty clients who take an interest in my cabinet. Perhaps I will tell a

white lie and let them imagine they are very likely fond-
ling a Shuzan and not a counterfeit. See that blue there,
I'll say. Shuzan's blues have a tendency to grow colder, to
veer toward violet, while the red veers to orange: it heats
up!

And then I will tell them how Shuzan's lacquer—its
recipe lost for centuries—cleaves to the soft cedar wood,
transforming it into something else, perhaps immortal,
cell by cell.

On the way home, we stopped for an early dinner at a new
restaurant Taka had raved about, Pearl Soup, its Japanese
country cuisine as good as any in Japan. The food was
great, as was the sake, and I found myself, who knows
why?—the sake, the happy mood we shared, my feeling
of deep affection for my wife—needlessly, shamelessly,
dropping a clue.

"Akiko," I said, "I must tell you, in fact I wonder how I
could have forgotten, but recently, a client—" Akiko
shuddered, if imperceptibly. I was thinking of the Cutter,
of course. "Lifted her knees—it was sudden!—and
revealed a pussy trimmed in the Brazilian fashion."

"Jesus Christ." Akiko squeezed her eyes shut and
shook her head as if to shake the moment off. "What is
this?" she said. "An epidemic? I mean isn't there some
movie—"

"I don't know. Is there a movie?"

"Well, yeah. Come *on!* It's notorious! For godsakes.
So—" I watched as my wife looked around the room,
despairingly. "Did you fuck her? Because. If you did. Well.
I'd like to know."

"Of course not! Do you think I—no! No!" I moaned in utter despondency although the affair singed the inside of my skull like a shovel full of hot coals. "I told her to *recover herself*—yes. Those—so absurd, really, were the words that came to mind. And then"—and here I dropped another clue, all the while wondering, why? Why was I doing this to a woman I cared for, I admired, a beautiful, talented woman, an exemplary woman?—"I held her. So like a child, really! As she sobbed."

"You *held* her?"

"As she sobbed, yes, you see—"

"You held her."

"Yes. She was feeling so humiliated! I—"

"You *hold* your patients?"

"Clients. Yes. Only *rarely*. Come *on,* Akiko!"

"Rarely. You've done this before."

There was no way around it but to lose my temper. "Don't persecute me!" I warned her. "I know what I am doing. I'm good at what I do. *I know the risks.* She was on the verge of suicide. The week before she had slashed her wrists. Her boyfriend found her, most likely just in time."

"I think you need to know," Akiko said, "how hard this is for me. And I will think of you now, in the new office, holding someone . . ."

"Ah. Akiko—no! Don't do this!" I sighed and thought: *I am a total fool. I really must do something about this weird—it is weird—compulsion of mine.* "The thing is," I continued, "you are right. I should not talk about this with you. It is unfair. But who else can I talk to? I mean—you are so *smart.* Akiko, you understand how people are; you are my dearest friend."

"Am I?"

"I have never trusted anyone as I trust you. And I guess if I brought this up it is because this woman, this really crazy woman, is the one I worry about above all. I think when she is stabilized, I'll be able to leave the practice for a week or two."

"You know how much I'd like that."

"Me too."

"I know how loving you can be," Akiko said, "how deeply you feel for your patients——"

"Clients. Yes. I do."

"Yes. I appreciate how important you are to all these people——"

"*Peculiar* people!" I blurted out with a sudden, over-whelming feeling of terror and disgust. "Sometimes I fear I am pissing my life away with peculiar people."

"Jesus," said Akiko. "For godsakes——"

9

I SCRIBBLE THESE NOTES between clients; I have fifteen minutes or so each hour except for the occasional trip to the can and lunch on the fly; I often write during the brief break I take for lunch.

What is curious about writing all this down is the fact that I find myself tossed into the memories of things I had completely forgotten, from infancy. These memories are like little theaters of the vanished self, sometimes frozen in time as beneath ice. Today I recalled a recurrent dream I had in early childhood. I had heard the phrase, "the land of milk and honey;" it was a joke as I recall; my mother and her sister had just come back from shopping at some favorite store that my aunt referred to in this way. These words of hers caused tremendous excitement. I begged to go there. I pleaded as my mother brayed with laughter and slapping me on the knee cried: *you damned fool!* Her sister, Loll, of kinder disposition, said, Oh darling, darling, it's just a joke, it's not like that at all—at least not for little boys! Why not? I wept, why can't I go there? Loll, who was a good sort, said O.K. We'll take you today. Right after your nap.

I couldn't sleep. I was wild with excitement. What would the place be like? I understood it was no *land,* but a shop, but meant for women, not for children or men. A woman's sweet shop! A teahouse, maybe. My daydream began this way: imagining a palace of a kind packed with glass-fronted cabinets full of ices and milkshake fountains—the ridiculous dream of a little boy who longed for sweetness, poor, miserable wretch that he was!

At last I was allowed to leap out of bed. My face was washed and my hands, my hair brutally combed, Loll (I have no idea what her real name was) benignly beaming. (As I recall, Loll was not very smart. The odious would make her beam. She laughed at my mother's jokes. Her gifts were always disappointing. Neglected as soon as they were unwrapped.)

The thrilling rotating doors. Their highly polished brass. And everywhere the smell of women. A rich perfume almost overwhelming. I may have sneezed. The smell of powder so rare these days and the perfumes rosier than now. Far sweeter, far too redolent of mothers and their sisters and friends and yet intoxicating—as was Loll's indivisible bosom, weighty as a watermelon.

There we were. It was a palace devoted to women's clothing. Not a cookie in sight. Only the infinite air, a female ocean. My mother brayed: *Look at his stupid face!*— her laughter bouncing off the countertops like spheres of glass. It was a lesson, one of many. In this way I was trained to despise all my dreams.

I was bred to anger, born and bred to rage. I eat away at the ripe flesh of things like a wasp eats away at the body of a fig, leaving it to rot. The longing for, the hatred for all the lands of milk and honey—those recurrent vipers rising up to sting me on the neck. Every endeavor taken, every optimistic gesture deflated and compressed by my mother's teasing: *Off he goes again! To the Land of Milk and Honey!*

This is what I learned: I was not intended for delight. Delight was made to elude me.

This is what the parent does: he yokes the child's lion to a chariot and sends all his elephants trumpeting off to war.

The child is born speaking the languages of birds; the child has horns and scales and wings; it has a beak; it has a cloven hoof. He is the sum of all creatures: the ones that swim, the ones that soar, the ones that leap, the ones that maze the earth with burrows.

If I have chosen to take my war directly back to the womb, can you blame me?

I am the spirit of negation. My aspects are twinned. I am attraction and repulsion. In this way I turn inexorable. I am a wheel. As I rise, Sweetheart, I carry you along with me, a heady, dizzying spin toward the sweet oceans of eternity. On wings of flames we sink into the sea of love. May we burn forever like bees in honey. Who does not wish for that delirium to last forever?

When we fuck my darling, my kitchen, my cherry, it always seems the endless chain of causality has blossomed into bliss.

Why? She always wants to know, *why can't we stay like this forever? We have found the One Real Thing! Is it not the Highest Good?* When I turn this way and that, when I wrap my legs around you, have we not received the Most Perfect Knowledge? Is this not deliverance? Is this not Eternally Existing? Is this not the Nature of Happiness?

10

But always the clock strikes. The knife falls. In love I am only blind. There is no knowledge there. No purifying fire. A moment's bliss and then: the mule brays.

In the shadow of the wheel, nothing can persist. The shadow of the wheel is named Calamity. It is named: Contagion. There, nothing has significance. Nothing is real. Nothing visible; there is nothing to express. Beneath the wheel rage has rendered everything perfectly flat.

In the end I am like Death Himself with a scythe of ice. Yes, that's it: my blade is like the ones Eskimos were said to make of ice in the polar regions. There is the story of the Eskimo who makes himself a knife out of his own excrement because *it is all he has.* And it is as sharp as steel.

I think I am like that Eskimo. I live in a wasteland and yet I survive because I own a knife of shit.

11

THE WOMEN I SEE *come to be seen.* I offer the chance, perhaps the last chance, to be visible.

One sees one's self through the eyes of the other, and if the parent sees their own monstrous infancy, their own collapse, in their child, well then, that child is lost.

So when my beautiful client the Cutter, striped and spotted like a feral creature—she both loathed and worshipped that sweet body of hers—revealed herself to me (who knows? Perhaps she saw the movie, perhaps not—no matter. I have not thought to see it myself), she wanted to be *fully visible* and could imagine no other way, no better way. I only gazed at her that first time; I drank her in. She asked:

"Why are you so quiet?" I said:

"I am eating you with my eyes. And they are dumbfounded." She laughed at this.

"Why only with your eyes?"

"Because the pleasure of looking has turned me to stone."

"You're *hard!*" she said, still laughing. "And that is the point I wished to make."

"Hush."

I suppose you could suggest the Cutter was the beginning of my downfall. Until that moment I was always the one in charge. No longer. I cannot explain why this was so. Perhaps I had fallen in love. Whatever it was, I had fallen. Her sex was like a beacon at the end of a tunnel—or so I imagined. In fact, her sex was the tunnel I had always dreaded, always fled. If my mind was already treacherously mazed, she confounded the problem. She squared the maze and then she squared it again. I was now in an inescapable place although at the time I did not know it. When one is snapped up in the beak of desire, one knows nothing but fire. I hung suspended from that beak for days, weeks, months. Never have I been so taken by a creature. She was, I see this now, deranged, shrill, mundane. She was also stunning, quick, agile as an acrobat, shameless, and smart enough. And because she was always on the verge of self-destruction, she kept me on my toes. My habit, until then, calculated in its risk taking, became perilous, an addiction. I was needing to disrupt the Practice, to leave the house at odd hours because of my imperious need for her and because of her incessant breakdowns, hospitalizations, tearful calls from dangerous bars; once she was so drunk she could not stand; once she called to say she had cut herself so badly she came close to passing out, and awakened us in the middle of the night. Akiko was the one to pick up the phone. She passed it at once to me.

"A patient," she said. "She sounds really . . . drunk?" Angry, fearful, this and more, I feigned impatience, disgust. But I was in grave danger. The Cutter was shouting and I feared she could be heard. Shouting and sobbing uncontrollably.

"This is an emergency," I whispered to Akiko. And of course it was. I told the Cutter I was on my way. I dressed in slacks, a linen sweater; until then the Cutter had seen me only in suits. I sensed this would change the direction our affair was to take: the drama, my sandaled feet, the escalated risk, my wife's stark and troubled look.

"Might she be violent?" she asked, pacing the room. "What if she tries to hurt you?" But I knew that whatever the circumstance, the Cutter could be soothed by extravagant fucking. It was my habit to toss her about with a practical and tender ferocity; we were like two demons, droll and terrible together. I knew that in the early hours of the morning I would soothe her, bandage her, bathe her. Silently, in slow motion, in a sepia dawn, we would cleave together like Shuzan's lacquer to the soft cypress body. That when we came together, we would be healed of all the wounds inflicted upon us, the father's monstrous dick, the mother's ingenious tortures, all the theaters of horror that tormented us both, lost, hungry souls that we were, my client and I, mirror images of one another, raging like feral wolves beneath the bitter moon, the all-devouring mother moon, her horns up both our asses.

The sun would rise, she would be soothed, I would be soothed. She would cease to sob, weep silently at times, then cease her weeping altogether; I would feel her loosen up; I would feel her let go. I would feel her throat between my fingers pulsing with the orgasm, and she would sigh and sleep like a little child nestled in my arms.

I, too, would sleep, if only for an hour; I would shower; I would dry my hair; I would return home briefly to reassure Akiko, Akiko who had spent the night waiting for my call; I would have to make up a good story about the hospital, the dreadfulness of it all, the difficulty of leaving my client, if only for a moment. All that . . .

12

NAKED, THE CUTTER APPEARED to be sleeping on the floor. I could see at once that she had not hurt herself, but she was very drunk. There were marks all over her body, and as always the sight of them stunned me. She looked like a kid sprawled as she was, a shameless, crazy kid. A kid up for adoption. A kid up for sale.

I had the distinct impression that she was only pretending to be asleep and that she knew I was standing there looking at her. I think she knew the sight of her naked body ate into me; the Cutter leeched me. There is no better way to say it.

It was beyond the middle of the night. I slipped out of my clothes and tenderly roused her with my tongue, my teeth. *Ah, Kat,* I breathed. *My own Kat, your blue latex, your violet moss, your bitter lime* . . . She laughed her dizzying laugh; she said:

"So . . . it's *you.*"

It began slowly, a novelty for us. I knew what I was doing was disgraceful and relished that knowledge. Each time I kissed Kat's scars I knew I was wounding Akiko. *Unspeakable,* I thought, and it was thrilling. The Cutter in love is enigmatic. This is because she is imagining violent acts, staggering, terrible things.

And now she begins to complain, to enter into battle. I feel her nails tigering my neck and shoulders.

"Go easy," I whisper. "I'm a married man."

This simple fact enrages her. I have forgotten my promise to her, that I will stop sleeping with Akiko. When she tears herself away, cursing me, I say:

"You know I can't totally stop fucking her. I live with her! It's not easy for me, Sweetheart." And then she does something that frightens me. She slaps my cock; she slaps it hard. And then she slaps my face.

———

I found Akiko asleep by the phone with her head on the kitchen table. She looked so vulnerable, so lost, that I felt overwhelmed with shame. Or perhaps it was anxiety.

I covered Akiko's shoulders with a blanket and went upstairs to shower. I can never get enough hot water. So much filth and always the desire to scald it off. I thought I would stay under the water until the years spilled into the sewers of the city and I was new again. But the knowledge that I had to find a way to safely break with the Cutter had me crouching in a spasm of pain. It was an old pain, the pain of a prisoner who has been tightly bound with wire and abandoned in his cell.

As the burning water thundered down, I continued to crouch, wondering about the lethal necessity of sex, that murderous, that inescapable . . . and then I imagined that I was an insignificant thing spinning about in the vast sea of first things, irresistibly driven into splitting in two. I imagined that act as inescapable as the impulse to orgasm. I thought I had discovered the first instant of orgasm, there at the heart of things, at the world's beginning.

But Akiko was rapping on the shower door, peering into the steam and down at me. "My love!" she cried out in fear and wonderment, "My love!" the glass door open but a crack, her face floating above mine pale as the moon, "What are you doing? Are you O.K.? *What are you doing?"*

Akiko was hazed in steam, dripping with moisture.

"I'm worried about you," she said, and pulling her fingers through her hair: "I'm worried about us." I turned off the water and, grabbing a towel, laughed.

"I'm all right! I'm just all knots—I can't believe I spent the night at the hospital—what time *is* it? I'll be late—"

She said: "You haven't slept."

Seeing her so lost, so despondent, I gave her a quick squeeze—

"We're all right," I said. "Akiko. *We are all right."*

I dashed about scowling, drying myself with ferocity, dressing in haste as she looked on, wide-eyed, her arms crossed over her chest as if to hide her heart.

"Let's meet downtown for dinner. I'll call you from the office—" I pecked her cheek—as she once joked: *a poor excuse for what she craved.*

In the car I wondered at the brevity of things, recalling how Akiko had once consumed me utterly, how I had trusted her vivacious intelligence, a certain quality, a luminosity I revered. There was a time I thought her superior to other women. I told her she was the one who had *uncorked my bottle.* And in response to her confusion explained:

"I was once a little child who was turned into an imp so nasty he was made very small and put into a bottle, a sealed bottle, without any food or air inside; the bottle was a perfect fit."

13

THIS MORNING, FOR THE FIRST TIME, I drove to work in the car. A prehistoric Studebaker, it really should be scrapped, and yet I can't seem to part with it. The car is so much like me: once remarkable and now less so. The car is defective, it needs constant attention, it is calcified, cranky. But despite its defects, it is the only one of its kind out and about, and so I suppose in this way remains remarkable, somehow exceptional. If I took him in for a paint job he'd look a whole lot better. He guzzles gas. Akiko has suggested I replace him with a hybrid. A reasonable suggestion, yet I prefer not to be overdetermined by the current trends. My Studebaker is not easily classifiable. Like my clients, he is unstable. I feel a certain ambivalence about him. He appeals to me. He keeps me vigilant. He manages to call attention to himself. The Cutter thinks he is wildly attractive, touching: "I mean he needs a paint job, a little new chrome, and then, *wow!*" She, unlike my other clients, has seen him; I'm so often at her place when Akiko is away. I feel this knowledge of him adds a touch of coziness to an otherwise often tumultuous and even downright scary affair. He is a reminder that I am "safe," old enough to be her father, established, accountable, a professional, trustworthy, *her doctor.* Today, she will see him parked out in front of the new office.

When I bought the Studebaker, it was a major step toward the construction of an operative persona. He was remarkable but not showy. Subtly sexy. Not precious, nor flamboyant.

A Studebaker is not a car chosen by a fetishist or a gambler. It suggests a healthy and productive life. It is not the car of a survivor, or of someone overly meticulous. It is not the car of a voyeur. My Studebaker taught me how to dress. He was my mirror and perhaps he still is.

Except that I do need to take him to the shop for an overhaul, long overdue!

14

The new cabinet.

⁓

I wait for the Cutter.

⁓

As I wait I wonder about the world beyond my immoderate interstices. I mean the so-called "real" world, the world of everyday. The world of novelties and embalmers, anesthesiologists and escalators. The world of paper, paste, and cocktail hours. Public attention. Akiko's world.

I wonder what it would be to be unsevered from the instant, undiminished, as is she, intact. To live in Eden, before the smack, the disorder to which one is eternally espoused. (And even this *before* the father muscled his way into . . . but I will not *go there!*)

As when an adolescent, one entered into a moment of grace, riding a rented horse across the city beaches in the raging sun of summer, brown as a savage man, proud of the body I had suddenly grown into. Salt on my tongue, the wind thick in my hair—I felt the bounty of the world. And I knew that *I was of that bounty*.

Later, the university years, those distant evenings when I sat talking with friends over coffee—a thing I am less and less able to do; I wonder why? I have of late, grown increasingly impatient with language and all the rest. I suffer a general irritation with Akiko's damned *thingness*. I think: how dare she inhabit time as though she were the apple of its eye? Ah. I am tired of marriage. A house full of carpets and books. Instead I long for my clients, those

CREATURES OF DARKNESS!

They drift in the city air like pages from a charred book. They cannot live out their lives. They die young of famishment; they suicide; they are gnawed to the marrow of their bones by AIDS. (The risk! The risk of keeping such close company!) So unfathomable when one is used to the world as it was, and not so long ago. A spread table. The endless feast.

Once, in a European museum, Akiko pointed out a series of anamorphoses and their cylindrical mirrors. Painted on paper, they were incomprehensible, an ugly spill of color. But when one looked at their reflections on the curved surfaces of the mirrors, they became fully visible. And they were erotic. Shamelessly so. They were beautiful and they were obscene.

I am like these. My tribe is like this.

15

THE CUTTER IS LONG AND LANKY; she's like a hungry bone. She wants more from the world than she will ever get. She is striking, but in that she is not alone. She has a temper hot enough to fry an egg.

I can see at once that the new cabinet threatens her. For one thing, it further establishes me in my life. It is the demonstration that I intend to see more clients. That I do not intend to cut back my hours. It is likely we will spend less time together.

She is impressed but also outraged at the expense. Yes, I am certain that is so. I have not been particularly generous with her. She begins to resent this. They always do. Sooner or later the interstices are too small for everyone.

She is standing in the middle of the room. As I am seated, she towers above me in very high-heeled sandals and a silk dress the color of bruised plums. Her auburn hair, sparked with red, sets her face on fire. She says:

"I can't remember a thing. Was I awful?"

"You were *very* drunk."

"I *was* awful."

"Why were you drunk? That's the question you need to ask yourself. Why now? You've been doing so much better."

"So you say."

"So you've told me."

"So why do you believe me?"

"You're right. I could be deluding myself."

"I thought you weren't supposed to do that."

"I'm not. Kat. Sit down." She settles down at once, her feet curled beneath her and I know her heels will leave their mark in the new leather.

"I want more from you."

"I want more for you, too." I say. "But not in the way you mean. You know that is impossible. As much as I adore you, Kat." She glares at me. I continue.

"I think you are wanting more from everything, not just me. You *are* better. You need more room. It's a good sign, this wanting of yours."

She snorts. "A good sign!"

"These reversals are inevitable. You know this. Recovery isn't a linear process."

Kat bites her lip and begins to cry. "I want to die. I'm . . . I want to die," she repeats.

"Sweetheart," I say, rising, going to her, pulling her to me so that she collapses, shuddering in my arms.

"You talk about . . . about ideals, universal ideals . . ." she weeps noisily, extravagantly, "you talk about my . . . my autonomy . . . my . . . my self-determination. You taught me those words! But you don't mean—"

"Of course I do. It's all true, Kat. Our work together, our extraordinary love affair, they are all about your coming to terms with your past, your fear of love! Please, Sweetheart! Don't forget everything we've talked about, all the—"

"I'm fucking goddamned guys in bars!" she shouts. "I'm fucking all the wrong guys! I'm more fucked up than ever!" Tearing herself from my embrace she screams so that someone in the dental office upstairs hammers on the ceiling. I should never receive the Cutter during regular business hours.

"You twist everything into . . . into . . . any shape you want. And now! And now you want to get rid of me!"

"Have I said that? Have I ever said—Kat! You must stop this!" I point to the ceiling where the hammering persists.

"Look at you!" she glares at me. "Look at you! *Clenching your teeth!*" Grabbing her bag she stands up, having come to some horrendous understanding. Facing me, she says a thing that in another world would have turned me into a block of ice or salt or granite:

"I am *not!* I am not going to die to get you off the hook!"

"What are you talking about?" I whisper. "Where is this coming from? Who is talking about dying here? I—" I struggle for breath. I fear that the Cutter is threatening the entire edifice: Drear, Spells, the New Spells, the park, the house, the marriage, my reputation. All of it.

"Kat," I implore her quietly. "Sit down. We must talk. We must trust one another. You came to me for a reason. You were on the verge of self-destruction. But now—and yes! I know your tendencies to self destruct are still haunting us both. *Becoming is a fearsome thing!* But you *are* better. And this because of the courageous, the exemplary work we have undertaken together!"

Now she is perched on the edge of the psychoanalytic couch that has served us both so well in so many unexpected ways. In a seemingly infinite—I think: *how infinite the choreography of erotic encounter!* I can tell she is thinking along the same lines.

"Yeah. Well. O.K.," she says at last. Looking into my face she smiles. Kat's smile is winning. Sensuous and slightly askew. "It's true," she decides. "I'm not empty the way I was. I'd be O.K., maybe, if I could stop drinking. You know?"

16

You fill a house with precious things; they break. You fill a heart with precious things; it breaks. In the end it all breaks. All night long I hear bones snapping. My nights are my star chamber. In my dreams the elusive sweetness of the world is just around the corner: up a tree, waiting in the silver tower, at the top of the mountain, in a box secreted at the bottom of the sea, in the flame of Aladdin's lamp. And always between these legs or maybe those: the divine secret of sweetness.

Is it, I wonder, the same sweetness that seizes the fish when it spills its sperm. And the tigers when they fuck? The serpents as they coil and uncoil, thrashing in the mud together? Could it be that this elusive sweetness is at the heart of everything? Coupling, striving for delight. As once in Tahiti, Samoa, such places—

17

LATE IN THE DAY I received a call from a man named David Swancourt, a young man most likely, with an unusually engaging voice, disquieting, restless, intimate. Intrigued, I played his inquiry over a number of times before returning his call. I managed to reach him at once and we made an appointment for the following Friday in the new office.

Then: a shower (the downtown Spells has both a private shower and a restroom for clients, a luxurious restroom like a picture gallery), a nap, and a call to Akiko to discuss where we would meet.

One thing I am compelled to do, because it promotes coherence, is to take Akiko to a restaurant *where I have eaten with a lover*. Or in a risky part of town where I have engaged, if briefly, with marginalia. To be healthy one needs to bring the disparate parts of one's puzzle together and in this way defuse prevailing habits, promiscuity's fevers. At the same time it provides proof for myself and my wife—who labors beneath the weight of the clues I have inadvertently left in her path—that our life, hers and mine, is *singular,* is the *real one,* the one that *actually matters,* so that the clues are disarmed and whatever pain she feels anesthetized. Or so I intend.

I was wanting the Red Dragon, a funky place she dislikes. I like its shadows, its intimacy; I like its dragons; above all I like the fact that I had been there with the Cutter a number of times. I liked the risk of this. She lives nearby and came often; I knew I was pushing things. I said to Akiko,

"I wonder if you would be up for the Red Dragon?"

"O, *god!*" she said. "You know I never am."

"Last time you said the dumplings were O.K.—"

"We could go to the Vietnamese," she countered. "We both like the Vietnamese." I thought it over. The waitresses there were wonderfully attractive. There was a time when I had been involved with one. I could never decide if it was sex she wanted, or a father, or a green card. She did want money. A beauty with expensive tastes. I recalled a pair of boots she asked me to buy for her. Over a thousand—

"Are you still there?"

"I'm thinking," I said. "The Dragon's spareribs are in the Dragon's favor. They have that soup you like."

"You are impossible," Akiko said. But she was laughing.

We pulled into the parking lot at almost the same moment. Akiko looked great; she was wearing silk jeans the color of pewter and silver sandals with what must have been a four-inch heel. She was wearing a white silk sweater. I could see at once that she was a little nervous. She's no longer the person she was. She's watchful. She notices now when I look at women. For that matter, she notices pretty women often even before I do. She has developed a flair. It used to be she was secure in her own beauty. I dislike this insecurity of hers; it has made her less lovely. She enters the restaurant looking fretful. Lovely, surely, but fretful. Yet she used to like pretty women. She was one of their tribe. Now she resents them.

The Cutter is very pretty. As we enter the Red Dragon, the Cutter, who has been sitting in the shadows in the back, sees us at once. It's uncanny. It's as if she has been waiting there. She walks toward us and she calls out: *Doctor!* And being the bitch she is, she ignores Akiko and gives me a hug. I can feel Akiko wired, thrumming with anger and fear. When I introduce them, Kat barely glances at her. She knows she holds the heat. The moment lasts ten seconds but it seers Akiko just as if the door of a furnace had suddenly blown open. When we sit down I shake my head and say,

"A client."

"Now I've *seen* it." Akiko looks totally lost.

"It's a long process," I tell her. "And as much as I'd like to, I can't control every aspect of this. She's a rude person. Not a good person. Pretty impossible, in fact. She had no right . . . I'm *sorry,"* I say. "This has upset you. Me too. But Akiko. It doesn't *mean* anything. The meaning is here. Between us." I take her hands in mine and put them to my lips. I kiss her hands, her fingers, and then I put them to my forehead. When I feel her little hands against my forehead I think that if I knew how to weep I might have wept at that moment. The oddest thing.

Yet this reassures her. Perhaps this is the thing that keeps us going; Akiko is so easily reassured. So eager to trust me. It doesn't make any sense. But she relaxes; I feel the tension in her hands melt away. In a moment she is caressing my face. When I open my eyes her own face is open. Her eyes are tired, but their expression has softened.

"You once told me," she says with real sweetness, real heat, "that I stung your face and hands."

"And tongue."

"I want . . . I want to sting you again."

"And you shall, my love," I promise, "once this difficult passage is over."

When our food arrives, I notice the delicacy with which she lifts her dumplings, one by one, with her chopsticks. The delicacy of her perfect teeth, her mouth; the delicacy of her face. Why does the sight of my wife eating dumplings enrage me?

When the very air within one's marriage grows thin and dim, there is nothing to do but set out to find a richer, brighter air. When the glass is fractured, a new glass must be procured. These days my wife does not know what to do with her tenderness.

If I were Akiko, I'd be out fucking men.

18

HOURS PASS IN DREAR. I attempt to extricate a client from a life lived leaping from one frying pan into another. After she leaves I suffer the professor who is exhausted by absolutely everything. All that civilization has to offer: markets, dumpsters, embalmers, highway patrols. I recall something Akiko said the night before:

"I wonder why it is the animals, the birds and fish, manage to live so much more gracefully than we do. And now we are killing them all off. And soon there will be just people like you and me, and all that simple grace will be gone from our lives."

And I said this terrible thing. I said: "No one will miss it."

But now I can see her point, because I have no choice but to suffer the professor's fearful and sinister stories, fearful and sinister because they recall the acute, the suffocating misery of my infancy. As of late, I enter Drear with a dire sense of foreboding. I have come to dread the professor, whose visits are as chilling as a visit to the morgue.

Beyond the French doors, off in the distance, I see Akiko gazing into her beloved carp pond. And I envy her.

Then there are the hours in Spells, the elastic days, days rich in event, ripe with diversions. Days of figs and thorns. Yet Mr. Horner, as he must, returns home in time to sup. The wife across from him, a galaxy away, is hopeful, inquisitive, rich in beauty, promise, yet . . . I try her patience. I try her capacity to trust. I am her snake, she is my grass. She is vulnerable; when she breaks, all the king's horses and all his men will be unable to fix her. Should I smile, I would give myself away. Therefore I come to table scowling like a pirate. In this way the evenings pass.

"Why?" she mocks, "the dark look?"

"I don't like what I do." I think: You have failed to lick me clean of bile and brimstone and tar. *You have failed to release the Minotaur from his nightmare. I cannot forgive you.*

"What are you thinking? I feel like you are on the moons of Mars, or worse."

"Worse?"

"Another galaxy entirely."

"I am impossible to live with."

"I didn't say—"

"I am," I insisted. "Even I can't stand it."

The dinners follow one another; it's like being on an infernal carousel. She has grilled salmon; the fish has a crust of nuts; gilded like the helmet of a king.

"How do you do this?" I ask.

"I like to cook for you." Then, quietly: "When I looked in the mirror today, I saw that I am fading. I suppose this is why you are no longer eager to be my lover."

I was startled and knocked off balance by this bravery of hers. I had seen it before, but it had always taken me by surprise. I am not used to bravery. Not from men. Not from women.

"We can end this," she said simply. I took my time considering how to respond.

"I am troubled," I said hesitantly, searching for the right words, the right modulation, "in my Practice, it is the *Practice,* Akiko. Not you. Never you. You are exactly what I have always longed for." If I said this from need, love or from perversity, I do not know. "I am troubled in my Practice," I told her, Friday nipping at my heels, "and exhausted."

~~~~

Yet there are many evenings when I relish the quiet, when Akiko takes on a pearly glow like a fantastic creature born of the sea. In these hours the mystery at the heart of things exists exactly where we embrace, or read to one another, or walk together among the fallen leaves to the lake . . . and I suppose these are the hours that allow her to continue to give me the benefit of the doubt.

But is this any different, I ask myself, from what it was sometimes like with the Cutter not so long ago, when it seemed we were the children we had never been, she and I, on the verge of a great adventure. In those moments I could see what she saw: a vast, nebulous world just beyond the city's rim, a vaporous promise dazzling in the heat of my lust for her like a sumptuous mirage. But it was, after all, only a thing of shimmering heat, only an illusion briefly entertained, that under the impact of the day and its demands, her anger and her appetite, is dissolving now, at the speed of light.

19

DAVID SWANCOURT WAS SCHEDULED for the afternoon; already I had broken my rule for Friday, which was to keep the afternoon open for affairs of the heart. Over the years these varied from vivid to mundane.

Until recently, the Cutter had taken up the entire afternoon. We would go off together, to the coast or up in the hills outside of town. When Akiko was away, our Fridays extended into long, luxurious weekends.

Kat could be tender. She liked it when we could stroll together hand in hand like any regular couple. "What if?" she said on one of these marvelous interludes we shared in the interstices of our lives. "What if I am the one to domesticate Bluebeard?"

"Bluebeard!" I said, astonished that she could think such a thing of me, let alone say it with such spontaneity, even gaiety. "Whatever makes you think I am anything like that?"

"Oh, come *on!*" She stopped walking, and dropping my hand, turned to face me. "You *love* that filthy shit."

I was lost. I considered. I thought she meant anal sex. I said:

"You love it, too."

"Not as much as you."

"I thought you were crazy for it!"

"Are we talking about the same thing?" Kat asked, gnawing a cuticle, spangled in the sun.

"Maybe not."

"I'm talking about the videos, baby, the sick shit."

"Oh, god. *That.*" I felt at once as if my skull was being compressed. Even now, recalling this, the terrible pressure returns. It persists.

Before the Cutter I had never actually seen a snuff film. But early on in our sessions together she had insisted, for reasons still unclear to me, that I watch one with her. In fact, the first time I spent a night with her in her place, we had seen one, the first of many. The films had colored our affair and had, I can see it now, seeped into the hours and minutes of my life. Yes, such things can change the nature of time. Because the films were the unspooling of my most private nightmares. This is what the Cutter gave me. Free access to my own abyss.

In a session, one has access to the invisible. The visible presents itself in costume, with attitude. The client arrives dressed for the occasion, self-protective, guarded, hopeful, prepared to be seductive, wanting to be impressive, for her story to matter, to be unique; wanting her pain to be perceived as exemplary, important, meaningful.

Most often, a woman will arrive perfumed. Even if her heart has been torn from her chest, she will step into the office with freshly washed hair. Even if she is on the verge of suicide, she will present herself in her best shoes. She may question whether or not she should paint her face because she knows that if she weeps, she'll make a mess of it.

A guy will wear a clean shirt, a suit or tie; he may press his jeans. The first time the Cutter showed up she was wearing five-inch heels and jeans so tight I could see the swell of her mons pubis. In other words, she presented as a woman who was fuckable, and that her fuckability mattered to her more than anything else.

20

DAVID SWANCOURT BURNS into the cabinet like a flame, and when he leaves I will look down at the carpet and imagine it has been scorched.

Thirty-five. Tall, slender, a full mouth, an intense expression about the eyes. When he looks at me it's like having my genitals grabbed. A good, straight nose, good bones, soft brown hair cut at the shoulders; overall: a feral ease. A man who sighs. A man who paces, who steals across the room as though on skates. A man I cannot help but watch with a certain fascination. A man fully aware of his beauty. A man I find beautiful.

Unlike the Cutter, David Swancourt is enigmatic. Perhaps a chimera. There is a heat to him, a heat that matches my own. He reminds me of my youth, except for this difference: he knows about this heat of his, whereas I did not know, did not understand its implications, its possibility, until later. It took me two marriages to understand and acknowledge it; a third to follow its imperatives. I wish I had known sooner; I would not have wasted so much time. I would have been a smoother player from the start.

Yet, despite all this, I also see his insecurities. These, too, are like my own. I know he will tell me about chaotic sex, that like me he is driven to sex, that he is deeply humiliated by the imperiousness of this need, its rabid character; a need that bites and seethes and will not settle.

I know that he prides himself in his endless exploits, the *fact* of all the smoke and sulphur he has shared with so many, those countless others, each so different and yet, when push comes to shove, the same.

A body opens like a flower, like a wound beneath the assassin's knife, a street hit by a grenade.

———

This is how it was, even before the rest was revealed. I began at once to read him, to devour him with my eyes as he paced, this man so like myself, so fearless, so afraid, so famished, so incapable of nourishing himself. Above his left eye there was a scar that dove into his eyebrow; beneath it that eye of his tore into the room. It was an angry eye, a timid eye, an eye sucked nearly dry with fear. Unlike his other eye, the right one, the eye that showed how smart he was, how funny he could be, how playful, how inventive. His right eye was brown and brimming with humor. And then I saw that rarity: his left eye was blue. I marveled that I did not notice this at once. A cold eye, a hot eye. Here was one curious fish!

He had been pacing for ten, fifteen minutes. At last he dropped down into the other Eames. He said, "I have never been in a room like this before."

"How so?" He smelled of leather and citrus; he smelled of earth. I noticed his boots, a bit the worse for wear, caked with dry mud. And his fingernails needed attention.

"It's a beautiful room." He shook his head and, frowning, stood up. How he roamed about! How he wheeled and soared! Rose and fell! One minute a kestrel, the next a carp!

"Swancourt," I said, "is an unusual name. It seems . . ." As I searched for the right word, he returned from his wanderings and once again sat down. "*Unprecedented.*"

He laughed disdainfully. His gaze continued to drift. Each and every thing in the room caught his attention, but only briefly. And then he'd rip into me with those schizophrenic eyes.

He turned to the netsuke cabinet, and there he lingered. His profile caught me by the throat. There are faces that have the attraction of stars. Studded with star eyes, eyes that have a gravitational field. These are the eyes of those who are not only close to the edge, but who have already gone over the edge, perhaps cyclically, a chronic habit with them. And yet they have managed to return. The soles of their feet are scarred by fire; they have eaten glass; they have bedded down with snakes; they will do anything, anything at all to stop a certain kind of pain, which is the pain that comes to a person whose spirit has been so sullied and downtrodden the best it can do is shine forth fitfully, like a firefly caught within a fist, in the throes of a kind of final frenzy, and in the face of death.

These are the people who make for thrilling lovers. Invariably, their attraction is compromising. The risk is immense. But one is like them. One is willing to risk everything if only to burn brightly for a moment. The world is full of people such as this. People raging with hunger who may at any instant implode. Our planet is studded with such black holes. I have considered developing a cosmology of this ruinous eroticism.

David Swancourt was looking directly into my face.

"I think this room is too beautiful for someone like me."

"Perhaps not beautiful enough," I said. He pointed to his boots.

"I walked here from the bus station. I've left mud all over your carpet."

"I don't care," I said. "But you must be very thirsty." I stood up. "How about a Perrier—"

"A Perrier!" he laughed. Was he mocking me? I brought it to him nonetheless and watched as he polished it off thirstily. When the bottle was empty he set it down and, standing, said: "So. This is how it begins."

"It has already begun."

"Yeah," said David Swancourt, "I guess so. I'd say it has." For the briefest of moments he lashed at me with his yes with such unbridled ferocity I thought: *watch out!*

21

I RECALL, IN FACT I WILL NEVER FORGET, a brief event that took place many, many years ago when I was a boy of thirteen or so, watching my father get dressed for an evening out with Mother. His closet door was open wide and I could see his many pairs of carefully shined shoes, his numberless suits hanging on expensive wooden hangers, his ties suspended from some fancy sort of frame, everything clean, pressed, seemingly new, fussily cared for. I teased him and said, "Dad, you're some dandy!" (It was rare for me to tease; our family life was low on fun.)

"Dressing well is sexy, son," he said, "and do you know why?" He didn't wait for an answer. "Because when you step out of your clothes you're *really* naked."

This, I now know, was an emblematic moment. At the time it made me anxious, it made me blush, and even angry. Any mention of sex on my father's part always made me unaccountably angry. But then as I grew older, I found myself turning into a fussy dresser too, a man who wore expensive hats, silk suits and ties, tie-up shoes. And I discovered, indeed, how sexy this was, what a turn-on for certain kinds of women. And that it was, along with the fact of being an MD, considered both sexy and an indication of safety.

22

I BEGAN TO PREPARE for the momentous eventuality: David Swancourt's next visit. I prepare for a possible affair. I prepare for a possible affair as I always do. I buy clothes. I ask Akiko to come along because she has a good eye. And because it reassures her. It's domestic, the very thing loving couples do together. We do so little together. Me taken up with the Practice. My wife with her career.

Akiko makes no bones about what she thinks. "You look like a banker in that suit," she'll say. "I hate it!" Or: "You look like a public accountant." "For godsakes! You look like a serial rapist!" Inspired, she convinces me to buy a brown linen suit on sale; Armani. It's gorgeous, and perfect for early fall weather. The color of stale chocolate, it makes me look good.

"You look fantastic!" Akiko says. "I want you to keep it on and take me out for tapas *right now!*"

In this way I break it in. In this way I am prepared for David Swancourt's second visit.

I live in something like a heightened state. And yet also in a fog. While gardening, Akiko picks up a splinter. It is large and painful, but despite its size I am unable to remove it, my hands are shaking so. Instead I manage to stab her with the needle. It is almost as if the needle leaps of its own volition in order to wound her. *For godsakes!* she cries, *what is the matter with you?* I apologize and complain about my nerves; I promise to be very careful. When I stab at her again she is furious with me and perhaps, without realizing it, fearful. She no longer looks like the Akiko I remember courting so assiduously. She spends the next hour alone in the kitchen soaking her hand in hot, salty water, easing the splinter out bit by bit. I do not ask if I can help her. I go running instead. There is a full moon, and the trails are clearly visible. I like to feel my muscles move; I like to feel my body ache with movement. There is an eros to running. After all, one is running toward the future, the next encounter.

The encounter materializes as if cut out of the air. But this is ridiculous; after all, I had scheduled David Swancourt in. But there are people, you will have noticed, who astonish us, whose presence in the world seems miraculous. And David Swancourt is a creature of dream, or even a creature of dreamtime. What I mean is this: he entered the downtown cabinet as if conjured by a magic letter. As if he were the materialization of desire. As if he had been summoned by my fascination.

So: here he was again. Boyish, lithe, as edgy as a caged cougar, all of it. I thought: when David Swancourt enters a room, reason dissolves. The world begins to dream. I thought: this one is a woman. A woman coiled within a man the way a cock coils upon itself within a pair of silk panties. A beautiful woman—of this I was certain—about to surge from her shell. And then, as if he were able to read the progress of my thoughts, as if he had been reading my thoughts all along—and he had! He had been reading my mind—David Swancourt closed his eyes, almost as though he were keeping back tears, and in a whisper said:

"Ah. Shall I. Show her to you."

"Yes. Please."

"You will not betray us."

"No."

"Ah . . ." He sighed again, as if in a fever of his own. He said: "Watch this." So I did. I watched him rise up from the couch and stand before me. I watched in a joyous panic, although I did nothing to reveal my joy, nor my panic, but sat very professionally in my linen suit, forefingers pressed to my lips as is my habit when I am considering something very seriously.

"Look at me," he insisted, although I was. I said: "*I am.*"

"You are . . ." he waited.

"I am looking at you," I said.

⁓

And then almost imperceptibly, instant by instant, atom by atom, flame after flame, I saw him changing. It seemed every particle of light in the universe was careening toward him, this shimmering youth who was in the process of shedding his skin like a garment that fell to the floor only to pool among the shadows before dissolving altogether. Yet the room was free of shadows, but for the shadows he evoked and the darkness, like a heavy weather that rose up within me, or I was sinking into; I was sinking into a passion once again, except . . .

Except that when she stood before me now, naked but for a teal-colored string, her diminutive breasts studded with tiny sprays of silver stars that trembled as she breathed, falling like tears or foam so unexpectedly against her skin, I was overcome as I had never been before, of this I am certain, and gasped for breath, but only once. Which elicited a light laughter. She said:

"Don't move." She crossed over to where I sat and, leaning over, with her thumb caressed my cock strangling in my pants like a snake on a noose, and then, wheeling away: "Ah. But my time is up." And bending over, so that her ass was for an instant suspended within reach, took up her disguises and eclipsed out the door that leads to the back hall, the restroom, the street.

That evening my wife taxes me with strange questions apropos of nothing: she wonders why I call my patients *clients* and not patients.

"Because 'clients' is more democratic."

"Since when is 'doctor' and 'patient' classist?"

"Elitist, then."

"It makes no sense," she says. "I mean, the relationship between doctor and patient is exemplary. Almost sacred. For one thing—"

"The sacred has nothing to do with it. After all, my clients are paying for a service."

"So." Akiko speaks with a new bitterness. I perk up my ears. "In that way you are like a grocer. Grocers have clients. As do whores."

"More a whore than a grocer."

"Is that so?"

"Love, after all, is involved."

"Yes. I suppose that is so. Everything but kissing?"

"You hate me, then?"

"Do I have reason to?" She feigns indifference.

"You think I am a monster."

"It never occurred to me," she laughs. "Some monster! With only a single horn."

Suddenly I am overcome with weariness.

"I'm exhausted," I say, and standing with unexpected difficulty, make my way to the couch. Crossing the living room is like crossing the Sahara without water. The living room is dark, uncluttered, spotless; it is as if no one lived anywhere near it. As soon as I lie down I feel dizzy and heavy. I fall into sleep like a corpse into mud, wondering: What happens when a doctor sleeps with a patient? And the patient keeps paying the doctor for the other things they do together, the journey into pain and loss and mysterious crimes too terrible to recollect. Is the doctor, then, the patient's whore?

23

I keep shuddering. Something momentous has happened. Akiko points out that all the crows in the city have vanished. She has become watchful, strange. She finds a fish, one of her favorites, floating belly up in the pond. She brings up the shell again. The one she found broken, after I brought home that crazed shopgirl, Lucy. From an old collection, she tells me, and precious, because taken live from the sea a century ago. A thing now illegal because the species is nearing extinction. A perfect thing, until . . . Somehow the tips of its delicate prongs have been snapped off. As if, but this is impossible, someone deliberately snapped them off. But this is impossible.

"I was keeping it safe," she says. "A perfect thing. I mean a thing of perfect beauty. Beauty vanishes . . ." I feared she was about to use that terrible word: betrayed. And then it seemed to me that perhaps I had seen Lucy lift the thing from its box and before my eyes snap . . . Yes. I believe I recall seeing her look deeply into my eyes before pocketing—

"—the prongs," Akiko is explaining, "that keep the shell from being tossed about by the currents of the sea. The prongs that root the creature to the sand."

So that it may sleep as we all wish to sleep, undisturbed.
Had she really said that? Is this what I heard?

It is one thing to cover up one's own clues and another to remember to cover up someone else's clues, someone as erratic, as crazy, really, as Lucy.

"Let's go out!" I suggest to Akiko, to break the fog roiling into every nook and cranny of the house, "and shake off this dark mood. If we make a run for it, we could get to the theater in time. I have tickets; I actually have tickets—" I rifle through my wallet. "You know I sometimes get these little gifts—"

I have a need, such a need, to bring it all together, to ease the moment's terrible dis-ease. When Akiko agrees, I am greatly relieved. Yet the tickets had come from an old client of Spells; how these things haunt one's life! Yet there it is: things get solved but never really satisfactorily.

24

THE LITTLE THEATER on Third Street is not far from the
Crucible, so called, where all the night butterflies poison
the air with their breathing and beating of wings. Going
into the Crucible is like stepping into a pool of boiling milk,
and as we drive through I see one, a chimera, surge into our
lights before vanishing. Perhaps this is also David
Swancourt's world; it is too soon to know. And I realize that,
in fact, there is so much about him that I do not know.

The play is intimate, so intimate, and our seats so close
to the stage, that it comes across as being performed in
our laps. Akiko watches my ex-mistress avidly; I can feel
the static dancing on her skin. And the ex-mistress, having seared us both with one greedy glance, plays her part
with an uncalled-for ragefulness. But at last it is over and
we escape into the night air. Thankfully, the sky overhead
seems particularly expansive.

Akiko says:

"Who is the actress? Do you know her? It seemed like
she was aware of us the entire time. I actually picked up a
great deal of *animosity!*" Curiously, at that moment my
anxiety vanishes and I feel whole again.

"Well, yes. You're right. I wasn't sure at first, but I *do*
know her. Or *did*. She was once a client. I didn't realize she

was still acting. Gosh—she must be close to sixty. A very neurotic woman."

I know I should stop there, but something compels me to go on.

"A fascinating woman, talented, beautiful—although she looked haggard, I thought, tonight. I suppose that had to do with the role. Or her ongoing difficulties; I imagine she is still as unhappy as she ever was. A fascinating and unhappy woman."

I repeat the word "woman" purposefully. The word itself turns me on; I am stirred. I can grow hard just saying the word "woman" aloud. When I was a boy I was able to bring myself in the shower just by saying the word over and over. When I say "woman" around Akiko, I feel thrilled by the risk. "Woman" is another clue she hasn't yet fathomed.

That night after the play, after talking about the actress, I felt entire. I felt warm and secure and of a piece so that once we were in the car, I seized hold of Akiko and kissed her passionately; I would have fucked her then and there in the car in front of the theater if she had allowed me to. But she did not. The moment was lost and so it goes; this is one of the many ways a shared life begins to unravel, because then, when we had returned to the house and in the midnight driveway Akiko reached out to claim what was offered just minutes earlier, I pushed her away, oblivious to her rising anger and dismay, cognizant only of the mane of death, the stench of flesh roasting over coals . . . I stumbled forth alone into the house to fumble with the day's mail in its basket from Pakistan or who-knows-where, as if it mattered to me in the least.

Two

1

AKIKO IS WEARY. She is losing her luster. The force of his gravity is bearing down on her. These days she picks up splinters as easily as a cook picks up spoons; she bumps into things and trips on the stairs. The last time he looked at her he noticed the bruises on her legs and thighs. As young as she is, she begins to scowl; he catches her scowling unawares. He thinks it seriously impedes her beauty. Somehow it never occurred to him that one day she too would scowl, would join the scowling ranks he has left in his wake.

2

THE WORLD THEY SHARE is seriously shrinking. Perhaps this explains why he notices objects he had not noticed before. The room in which they eat is spare, but there is a statue of some kind on a stand in a corner and it casts a shadow that, when he looks its way, actually causes him physical discomfort. Which is ridiculous. Yet when he looks again, the malaise returns. To be precise, this shadow makes the skin on his scalp grow painfully tight, as though it were shrinking.

Akiko sits across from him. He notices how her lashes also project shadows; they scamper across her cheeks each time she blinks. The sight unnerves him. Her lashes seem longer, as does her face, the lines at each side of her mouth. And the shadows in the room. They, too, are longer.

Without a word, he rises and goes to the corner to investigate whatever it is that looms there. He finds an unfamiliar statue of oiled wood: a dancer of some kind with far too many arms. Hindu. She appears to be scowling, showing her teeth.

And her tongue! The length and breadth of his thumbnail, it seems to be thrusted at him aggressively. He says,

"Have I seen this before?" He picks up the statue and

examines it closely, as though it were an artifact from another world.

"Yes," she says, rising, and, sensing his difficulty, approaches him quietly. With real gentleness—where does this fund of tenderness come from?—she puts her arm around him. "Remember, we saw her together a while back in town and you said how much you liked her, so I went back and bought her and put her here. I wondered if you'd ever noticed! It amuses me," she smiles into his chest, rubbing her face against him, "how long it takes for you to notice these things. These changes I make in the house. Why is that?"

"I don't know," he says, full of wonder, somewhat stunned by this revelation. "I don't know if that is really true. Is it true?" he asks her now, almost as though he were a child, she thinks, needing her guidance. "I don't know why I once liked her so much!" he says, pulling away. "She's on the rampage." Akiko is bewildered. Hurt.

They stand together in the early darkness. They discover that they do not recognize one another. Frightened, she takes his hand and says:

"Come sit down. I've made something delicious for dinner." But she thinks: *So it has come to this. We have been reduced to this. But why?*

They eat in silence. She does what she can to keep back her tears. She has lost him, but she no longer knows whom she has lost. She believes she loves him, yet he is not the man she fell in love with. All the shadows in the room have now conspired to take him from her. She forgets to serve the salad. He neglects to pour the wine. As Kali dances in the corner, they sit alone together in a boneyard. Again she wonders *why?*

3

AFTER DINNER, Akiko puts on a heavy sweater and takes a walk. For some reason she remembers the first time they took a trip together. Oaxaca. Now that she thinks of it, his behavior had been incongruous, somehow immodest. They had only just arrived and there was so much to see, the city in the grip of life. And yet he must find a pen shop. Feverishly he began approaching strangers. Streets were named, directions given, and off they ran. He hurried on ahead of her, oblivious to the many things that caught her eye. In new sandals she trailed behind, the streets fraught and fractured, rubble at each step, as he sped on like a large cat, his own sandals as snug on his feet as those sturdy pads lions wear. Yet everything caught her attention, the town was a living hive! Why wouldn't he slow down and let her see it?

When they reached the shop, the display of pens was clearly unsatisfactory. He hovered above the sweaty glass case and asked to see them all. He fingered them, returning to an old one, stubby and thick, of indecipherable color. She and the shopkeeper looked on as her husband stroked it. A unique item, its pump unusually conceived. Its fat body held a lot of ink.

A glass bottle was now set out upon the counter, its label faded and flaking, its facets dulled with dust. She was losing patience; already so many precious instants had passed! Outside the hour was white, someone was singing in the air above them, and then: the sudden ringing of a vendor's bicycle bell. When she caught a whiff of coffee she remembered she was hungry; they had left the hotel without eating breakfast. Yet there her husband stood, unreasonably transfixed. She decided to complain, to insist that they move on for godsakes—an impulse thwarted by the uncanny intensity with which he continued to examine the pen. And although it was absurd, impossible in fact, what she saw in his eyes was sexual ardor.

Her husband was trying the pen's pump mechanism. Dizzy with bewilderment, she watched as the ink fountained down into the bottle and then as it was sucked up again. When he dabbed the pen's tip with a small square of blotting paper, she saw that the gesture was exactly the one he used after taking a piss, holding his cock in one hand and soaking up the last drop of urine with a folded tissue.

Tonight, as she wanders the woods in the moonlight, it occurs to Akiko that the pen shop had provided a public stage upon which her husband had sexually performed. That what had happened in the pen shop was a disclosure. An admission of betrayal. In the pen shop in Oaxaca, he had betrayed her before her very eyes.

Is it possible? Is the world as strange as this? No, she decides. It cannot be as strange as this.

4

IN THE MORNING he stands in the shower until something shifts, the dark weather that has begun to plague him dissolves; he rises like Neptune from the cleansing waters and feels beautiful; he touches the muscles of his calves and arms; he caresses his stomach and chest; he feels the comforting weight of his sex—and as he steps out into the sunny room and tiles to stand before a window facing east, he feels expansive; he thinks his home is like the palace of an Assyrian king; he relishes the comforts it provides. Even the towels, he notes with satisfaction, are luxuriously sized and of a rich, indeterminate color, like a warm sand of nacreous shells.

He has the dressing room of a prince, with a large three-way mirror that allows him to fully see himself. By the time he sets out for the new cabinet, he is his own man. He has once again set up the day so that by three he can receive David Swancourt without any fear of disruption.

He has rearranged the room. And opened windows. The distant roar of city traffic delights him. He is an urban prince at the height of his powers. A king of a kind. He is wonderfully strong, his flesh burnished like bronze. He is wearing a silk tie the color of burned oranges. He ranges through the room, delighting. Everything is renewed. Everywhere new buildings rising, old neighborhoods torn down, the dingy houses and their sorry little orchards replaced by mansions. There is talk of a new city park. The theater and library, the art museum, have all been recently transformed into temples, palaces! He thinks he lives in Babylon! He is the king of Babylon! Everything about his life is remarkable. There is a boundlessness to the day, to these rooms, this city, his own life, his own erotic hunger, this capacity of his to awaken erotic hunger. Spells is ready to receive his new lover in whatever form he/she decides to take. Perhaps David Swancourt's forms are limitless. He'd like to think so. This time he has found a lover as protean as the weather. As protean as he is himself.

This is what is delicious: a professional man, a trustworthy, mild-mannered, thoughtful man who measures his words; a beautifully groomed man of impeccable taste who moves with ease; a graceful man, a man whose mind is occupied by many obscure complexities, whose life is both comfortable, expansive, and above all mysterious . . .

5

. . . AND ALL OF THIS on the line. Reassuring, deeply desired. Because when it is set on fire, it blazes with such intensity! When such a man stands fully clothed but for his bounding cock, which she takes with such delicacy, such tender ferocity, into her mouth, well! Then the entire castle of cards so carefully set out upon the table tumbles to the floor with unprecedented abandon! And when the man and his life have all burned down to a small heap of ashes, well then, she'll dance upon those ashes, she will be Kali in a necklace of bone.

This is what drives David Swancourt: the burning of a world, the setting of a man on fire, a distinguished man, the man she can never be, not ever, because that chance was stolen from her during her own secret prehistory. He is the man she would have become, or so she thinks. Because she does not, cannot know, the bitter truths that rule him; she does not know, cannot know, that he, too, is in drag.

She does not, cannot possibly imagine, that her doctor is her biggest risk. Because she has come to him in deep trouble. Because a month earlier she went off with three men she picked up in a bar and was raped. Because like Kat, she drinks too much. Like Kat, she is drawn to those who will hurt her. Because she had come on to the men who had raped her. Because in some elusive country deep in her mind, she wants to be fucked into oblivion. Lovely Anna Morphosis! She wants to be fucked to death. Except it's not that simple. She has come to see him because she wants to live.

That week he had called her to ask her her name. *Jello,* said David Swancourt. *She's over her head, Doctor. She's in a bad way.* And her doctor. What did he say? He said: *Together we will make her O.K.*

6

JELLO CANNOT IMAGINE what a real childhood would be like. The glimpses she has had are so stunning, so sumptuous, so utterly desirous, she dares not engage them for fear of dying of unrequited longing. But sometimes she cannot help herself. Because these memories ground her. They remind her what it was like to be awestruck, to be giddy, to be joyously giddy with the world's promise.

There dwells within her a certain fragrant weather, a certain bright knowledge, a safe place where she can, at odd moments, be devout—worshipful in other words—of the mysterious process of living among others. When such a moment seizes her, she needs to share it; she needs to talk about it. And now, at thirty-five, she fears that if she does not talk about all of it with someone she can trust, it will turn to dust; she'll never be able to access it again.

A brass watch belonging to her father, her fascination as a little boy with watches, with small machines of all kinds. Before she became Jello, he was a mechanic. He liked to roll under cars and smell their hot, greasy underbellies. Because he was clever. Because he liked the way it felt to be close to the ground. Because when you are on the ground, flat on your back, there is no place to fall.

Because when he showered down after work and dressed in pressed jeans and a clean shirt, he felt good. He spent hours wandering the mall, days even, hunting down the right shirt.

One day it wasn't a shirt he bought, but a dress. The salesgirl liked him; maybe she was teasing him, or maybe she had a hunch. Or it was simply the fact of his beauty and she was curious; she wondered what this beautiful boy would look like in a beautiful dress.

The changing room was hospitable. Large enough for the two of them. It was an ark infinite with possibilities. In an instant they both vanished within its mirrors.

She undressed him. She showed him how a woman undresses a man. She fondled his nipples and she wouldn't let him kiss her. She said: *Just let me play!* She was droll, spunky, radiant. He was down to his briefs. She cupped his erection in her hand and said: *You have to behave yourself because you are about to become a lady!* When he laughed she hushed him with a kiss. He was riveted to the spot. The dress spilled over his body. After, he'd think about how they had found this little nest for themselves.

Because he was in a dress he felt he could be soft. He whispered: *Now am I your lover or your sister?* When she burst out laughing she was fired on the spot. The two of them were banished from Foley's. The months they spent together were the happiest of his life. They became bandits, stealing dresses for themselves, shoes, perfume, makeup. He would flirt with the salesgirls as she, in the midst of superabundance, would uncover and lift the rarity.

Understand that they were not ruled by greed, but by the need to be transformed. And of course, the need to risk the freedom they had just claimed for themselves.

Nevertheless, they were overturning the chaos that had from the start been an infliction. They transformed his tiny apartment into a clandestine backstage dressing room. They bought an outsized vanity from the 1950s, its mirror intact, and filled the drawers with makeup. They experimented with wigs. They might have gone on this way forever except that he fell in love with a man. For a few days they wept in one another's arms. Then it was over, and David Swancourt was on his own.

Jello changes her colors often. She shimmers. She does not want to be recognized, seized upon, locked up, and shut down. Her colors are lime, lemon, strawberry, blueberry, black cherry. She does not want to be harmed. She wants to flicker like the Aurora Borealis. She wants to be harmed. She wants to bleed like a severed aorta. She wants to be safe. She wants to be safe. She never wants to bleed again.

She goes to him because he is known to like trannies. He's seen scoping out the Crucible. He's intrigued more than he realizes. He once talked a he/she out of a sex change. He said: *The knife is just another way to flee pleasure.*

Ever since the rape she feels as though a grenade is about to go off in her head. She's badly boxed in. And what she recognizes about the doctor at once is that he is himself boxed in. Maybe she forgets why she is there. She decides to unbox him. He will be her jack-in-the-box. She will find the mechanism that will release him.

7

THE THIRD FRIDAY wheels into his life. It seems miraculous when Jello appears. She burns her way into the downtown Spells like an arsonist. When she enters the room, he rises, stunned by the extravagance, the totality of David Swancourt's transformation. Jello is absolutely gorgeous. He thinks that if chaos spins at the heart of things, David in his dress really puts a finger on it.

His astonishment is so evident, so transparent, Jello laughs, the illusion simultaneously shattered and intensified by the fact of David Swancourt's laughter. It's like the world's most fascinating shell game.

David Swancourt's laughter releases his own. He discovers there is nothing funnier than an extravagantly eroticized woman laughing like a man. Under the impact of this laughter, the world turns upside down and convulses.

She takes a step toward him. He meets her halfway between worlds. When they embrace a season passes, then another. Another season, another cataclysm. Neither of them expected this. They sleep, then awaken. The new Spells is deep in shadow. She grabs her things, she turns, says: *Hey*. And is gone. An act of devastating magic has taken place, and it is too damned late to do anything about it.

He is dizzy with a kind of murderous fury in the face of his own banality, the impossibility of the task ahead: to return home for dinner. He reeks of perfume, sperm, sweat; he showers like a maniac and changes clothes.

He likes what he sees in the mirror. He can pull this off.

He has this brutality in him that cannot always be masked. But it can never be measured, also, because it is mutable, in constant flux. Now seemingly playful, tender. Now an infection, dismay. His brutality is a source of joy and confusion, provocative, always. It resides in his marrow. When he is merely mischievous, well, it is a blessing.

His brutality is both fearlessly naked, triumphantly so, and at the same time deeply ashamed of this nakedness.

⁓

He calls Akiko to say he'll be at least twenty minutes late. She has invited friends for dinner, and this is far more than he is capable of. He offers to pick up some wine to buy himself some extra time.

"A Mascara would be great, actually," she says. "I'm making a tagine."

8

ON THE DRIVE HOME he decides that Akiko's ordered life is anomalous. He thinks: *I carry the tower within me.* An old story. An ancient story. A story inscribed in the Book of Nature from the start. The world was born in confusion, in confusion it proceeds, in confusion it will fall.

At dinner he is mostly silent. His wife's friends are artists—a photographer and a painter. The painter is clearly irritated by her lover's drinking, yet the drinker's insolence is amusing, and he is grateful he takes up so much room.

"This will lead to oblivion, if not a row," the painter warns.

Akiko laughs: "I hope he intends both for later."

"All heroes have their weaknesses," the drinker grins at his host and winks.

"What do you know of weakness?" he asks him. It is his first unsolicited sentence of the evening.

"*Everything!*" the drinker brags. "I collect vices as others do stamps."

"Such as?" The mood is changing. He can tell he is bringing an unexpected edge into all of this.

"Wine," he says, lifting his glass toward Akiko, who fills it. "Women." He nods first at Akiko and then at his mistress. "Song. But . . . I do not intend to sing."

"A blessing," says his mistress.

"I'd like to hear the man sing," he says with an implied belligerence he knows Akiko dislikes.

"Then *I will sing!*" the drinker declares, "in my host's honor!" He stands, knocking over his chair, struggling to set it on its feet again before belting out a piece of obscenity from *Carmina Burana*. When it is over, he bows and turning his back on them, makes his way unsteadily to the bathroom.

"Don't get lost!" his mistress calls cheerily after, retrieving crumbs of chocolate cake from her dish with her finger. He thinks: *Heavens be praised. The repast will soon be over.*

"It has been said," the drunk intones as he returns to the table, his fly unzipped, "that Dionysius manages better in the meadows and the woods than the living room."

"He is going to fall," his mistress decides.

"As the broads all fall for him," the drunk declares. "Or so he likes to think."

"Ah," the wayward doctor says, for he cannot resist: "A man after my own heart."

"Or cock," Akiko mutters, to the surprise of everyone. "A little joke," she whispers. She turns to him. "A little joke, my love. On me."

It is an entreaty. Or perhaps a warning. He wonders: *just what does she know?*

9

Saturday morning he feels such a tender longing for Jello, such an ache in every bone, that he calls her, breaking all his rules.

Sleepy, surprised by his call, he can hear a growing excitement in David's voice. He asks if he can speak with Jello. David tells him Jello *is not there,* but he expects her back *later in the day*. He suggests they meet downtown at four.

Until now, he has always been a cautious seducer. Now this caution seems precious, adolescent, absurd. He prepares himself for the day ahead, relieved that by the time he is out of the shower, Akiko is already at work, the studio lights blazing in what is a misty fall morning, overcast, mysterious.

He thinks: I am the Prince of Saturn, on a holiday on Earth. He leaves a brief note on the kitchen table, something vague about getting the car serviced. The old Studebaker justifies many absences. What's more, such banalities have a way of dispersing the stench of smoke. The next thing he knows, he is out and about, a leopard on the prowl. The world unfolds and time dissolves. It is ten o'clock in the morning.

He sees a cigar store where he has flirted, heavily flirted, with a woman like Lucy, not much older than a child. Impatient with fate, her dreams much bigger than her means, she has a way of revealing not only what her naked body looks like, but what she is like in bed. He cannot look at her without imagining plowing into her.

He sees her right away behind the counter. As soon as she sees him, she gives him one of her best hot looks. A customer leaves; he suggests they have lunch together, asks when she takes off for lunch. She is wide-eyed, exhilarated by this sudden outspoken interest. *Eleven,* she says. Perfect. Only an hour away. He imagines her co-worker watches this come together with envy.

He kills time with what Akiko ironically calls "domestic bliss": the bank, the drugstore, where he buys a carton of Kleenex in handsome bronze-colored boxes for the new Spells. When he returns for her, she is already waiting on the curb. He asks her what she's in the mood for.

She's a fantastic little tart; she simply reaches over and squeezes his crotch. He says: *I know just the place.* She says: *So do I.* As they approach the arboretum, she unzips his fly. There is a dirt road parallel to a new public road that circles far back into the woods and ends behind an abandoned gravel pit. They fuck like high school kids in a kind of frenzy. She smells of oyster mushrooms and won't stay still. She's showing off, eager to impress him. At some point he goes crazy with it and forces her ass. Things are out of control now; she is crying, fearful. This all goads him on. He tells her she's incredibly sexy, not to be afraid, but he's almost impossible to understand. He's thinking of Jello, of David Swancourt, both of them, the mad edge to fucking a guy. This kid, he thinks, is small, her body sweet and compact, except for her breasts, which are on the verge of unmanageable. And although he fully appreciates the ripe fruit of her, he is thinking of the length and sinew of Jello's thighs, and David's ass, so that somehow he is fucking David, Jello, and the kid at the same time and comes, howling, and she, the little imp, pretends to come too, hoping to save the day and with it herself.

10

SOMETHING IS ACCELERATING. His life is speeding up. This is an old feeling and yet there is something new going on, unfamiliar. The new room, too, is unfamiliar, and the netsuke all so strange, buzzing behind the glass in a new Spells all their own.

He takes out the erotic ones. They nest in the hand like a breast, the smooth heal of a woman's foot, a delicate ear or elbow, the head of a cock, its root, the testicles, that delicacy, that weight. He can understand why people collect these, why they are so rare, so coveted. And then he notices that *all* the netsuke, not just the erotic ones, have this quality—even the frog crouching on the body of the persimmon, the twinned gourd, its cut stem erect as a nipple, a wasp feeding on the cleft of a plum. He is like a voyeur, turning these over and over, examining their little dimples, secret moles, and discolorations. In his hands the netsuke begin to sweat. He thinks that the more they are fondled, the more they will be his.

An illicit Saturday like so many others. A Saturday unlike any other. He looks out the window at the weight of the sky accumulating just beyond the city limits. In the distance, the mountains are already obliterated by rain. The traffic hums; the river slides past in silence as it does always.

Four o'clock, and already it is evening.

He is seized by uncertainty. The seconds pass with a terrible slowness. It is like swallowing nails. *Perhaps she will not come.* Three minutes past the hour. His wife will wonder why he has spent the entire afternoon at the garage. Soon it will be winter. His wife will be without her garden. When she is not in her studio, the house will ring out with his absence. She will brood upon the clues he has dropped in her path like luminous stones. She will take greater note of his moods. She will taste another woman on his tongue.

The phone rings. He leaps on it. He says: *Yes!*

"It's me," Akiko says. "Don't I get to see you today? I thought you were going to the garage. They said——"

"I came here instead to read some notes. And fell asleep on the couch. What time is it?"

"Almost four-thirty. Don't forget, we're having dinner guests——"

"Again?"

"I don't see people all week. Not even my own husband."

"Am I being scolded?"

"I'm sorry. No! I'm *not sorry."* At which point Jello walks in. Incandescent.

"I have to finish up here," he says. "I won't be late. I'll pick up some wine. Some champagne." He looks on as Jello bends to the table and touches the netsuke he has left out.

"What are we celebrating?"

"Life," he offers.

"Yours?" she asks. "Or mine?"

"Jesus!" he laughs. "I *am* in trouble!" His laughter reassures her, or so he hopes.

"o.k.," she says. "No later than six. I need you to husk oysters."

⁓

Outside the rain begins and in a moment slams into Spell's high windows. Jello is nervously threading her hair with her long lacquered nails. They cannot kiss without moaning. He tears her blouse open. She is too excited, too triumphant to complain, although she is unsure how she will replace it. Or when. When the phone rings the room is darker, as if by necromancy, and the windows silvered with rain. Akiko wonders where he is. It is only just after six, but still . . . He puts down the receiver. *Shit,* he says.

"o.k., buddy. Time to close up shop, eh?" says David Swancourt.

"You make me crazy," he says. "You make me forget everything."

"You make *me* crazy, baby," Jello says, and the acute banality of this phrase, uttered first by him and now by her, terrifies him. He says:

"We have to get out of here a.s.a.p."

With a kind of tragic dignity, Jello stands, and carrying her panties and shredded blouse, all the rest, walks to the hall. In silence, they shower together, put on their clothes, walk out into the rain.

11

HE HAS CHANGED HIS CLOTHES for the third time that day. He is feeling unaccountably safe and renewed. He is an acrobat who has successfully walked a high wire in a gale. In the kitchen he kisses his wife behind the neck and at the table thinks he has never been more spontaneous, more brilliant. He talks about his Practice; he cannot let it go. No matter that the conversation rushes off in other directions. He always brings it back to the thing that matters: his good work with people, the way his clients flourish, the ways in which madness makes fools of the best of us, how fools become kings and assassins reclaim their innocence. The lives that split apart at the seams, the seas that bleed, the sons buggered by their fathers, the client who sees his thwarted life in every red light; how the world breaks apart only to reawaken, and demons cling for their lives to every star. Carelessness, exhaustion. What it is like to be marooned on an island of the mind. The car wrecks, the calls for help, the ones who drown, the ones who drink up an ocean before sitting down to dinner.

When much later he falls heavily to sleep, his wife notices that his heart is beating uncommonly fast.

12

Akiko lies awake next to the man who was once her lover. He sleeps as if nailed to the bed, his face so knotted with pain it is almost unrecognizable. How is it possible? His youth and beauty have dissolved. She looks at his face in the moonlight unbelieving, and faults herself for this indiscretion. She thinks that despite the stories he has told her, or perhaps because of them, always the same stories and always told in the same way, she does not really know him. Akiko is at a loss; she is in way over her head.

Sleep finally begins to claim her. Halfway there she wonders: *What is that taste of another's pleasure on your tongue?* A voice from her ascending dream answers: *Only death, brushing your lips with her wing. What is that sound?* she wonders, sinking into sleep. *Only the lid of the sky, only Death's eye, snapping shut. Why is it I do not know these things?* she wonders, dreaming now, beside him. She hears his voice, the beloved's voice answer: *Because I wanted to keep you safe.* In her dream she marvels: *Safe?*

When Akiko awakens, her heart is hammering. She awakens stunned to the quick by a dream. In her dream she goes to the new office alone and opens the netsuke cabinet.

They are gone; instead there is a vast collection of porcelain dolls, each only a few inches high, female, male, their genitals distinct. If their sex and the color of their eyes and hair varies, they are all otherwise identical.

That is to say except for one. Like Akiko's, her hair and eyes are black. But what makes her unlike the others is the gaping hole that pierces her belly where her navel should be.

It is close to four in the morning. Akiko rises cautiously and makes her way in the dark into the hallway; in the dark she wanders the rooms of their house unable to quiet her heart, considering her dream. Entering the living room she sees the phone light blinking. A message left while they were sleeping, a brief message for him. A woman wanting him to call. A woman who called in the middle of the night. She recognizes the voice of the framer's assistant. The one who spilled coffee on her portfolio months ago.

Perhaps it is true that catastrophes like to accumulate. Because Akiko now wanders in the chill air like a lost person, a homeless person, into the garden. When she reaches the carp pond, she sits down at the edge. In the distance at the world's end the sky begins to whiten, and she sees that all the fish are dead or dying. She wonders how lethal this contagion actually is, how far it reaches. She knows how far it reaches.

He sleeps unusually late. As he sleeps, she gets on with her life. She makes tea. She calls the gardener. When he comes they discuss what needs to be done. He is an old friend by now and sets to work at once. The fish must be

buried, the pond emptied, its pumps and rockery, everything, disinfected.

~

She pushes herself *through her paces*. And there is that other
funny American expression she likes: *keep on truckin'!* In fact
she is fighting for her life. When she looks back, all the
clues he has left over the years blink on and off like the
eyes of wolves in the dark of night. She decides to finish
the triptych. An act of will and an act of faith in her capacity to live in a world that is collapsing.

The triptych is nearly complete. Paradise. Hell to the
right, Limbo to the left. In the center, Eve, perfectly
human, is receiving a hand grenade from a Minotaur who
is clearly her own mazed husband. Her Paradise is a take
on the Paradise of Islam, packed with nubile virgins, but
also fantastical streetwalkers, temple whores, little girls,
the gods and goddesses of love, copulating creatures of all
kinds, lascivious boys, devastatingly gorgeous drag queens.
If these figures are all distinct up close, from a distance
they vanish, become a jungle of blossoms and extravagantly blossoming bushes and trees.

So, Adam, a Minotaur, dwells in a boundless harem. If
Eden matters to him, it is only because it is sexed. Her
Minotaur's sex is scandalously large, gorged with blood,
striking Eve's thigh. His balls, dark as plums, quiver
beneath. If Eve is aroused, creamy, her sex is folded into
itself, hidden. Only the cleft, like the mark on a plum, is
visible. And if Eve is eager to accept Adam's gift, it is only
because she is blindfolded.

~

When she returns to the house, he is gone and the girl's message deleted. On the dining room table, she finds a note. The car. The garage. So: the world has shrunk down to this. This all-encompassing banality.

Later, much later when he returns, the Studebaker washed and waxed as a proof of a kind, of what? His fidelity? She tells him about the pond, the lost fish.

He is feeling generous, expansive, on top of the world. To his own astonishment he recalls that she had bought the fish in San Francisco. *We've been talking about a break,* he says. *Why not go to San Francisco? A long weekend. You could choose the fish you like.*

"You know what I think?" Akiko says.

"No, Sweetheart, I don't."

"I think you are patronizing me. *Sweetheart.*" He hates her for this, and if he wonders what she knows, he does not ask. As for Akiko, there is so much she wants to say, but does not. So much she could ask, but will not. She has received her dream as a revelation. She knows that his lies are boundless, that he lies as he breathes, by necessity.

⁓

That night she roasts quail. Over dinner they circle the abyss like cautious lions. He tears his birds apart in his hands like a hunter from another century.

13

AFTER DINNER she takes her car, vanishes, tries to make sense of the city, tries to relearn how to think. He stays behind in the house and for a time stands looking out at the trees, at the beauty of the trees stirring mysteriously in the moonlight. He decides to write Akiko a letter. He is not convinced he wants to lose her. He is not relieved by her anger but forlorn. He dislikes the feeling.

He writes:

I have to acknowledge a certain disorder within my erotic life. Or I should say sexual life, as the erotic impulse seems sorely compromised at this time. That is to say I am driven to sexual encounters, but joylessly, without élan, *without* delight. (But how true is this? he wonders. No matter; he persists.)

Akiko, my love, I cannot bear to be touched by you, to touch you, for a number of reasons. For one, I fear if we touch you will know how compromised I have become. How filthy. I believe my body's texture has changed and I am certainly colder. There are times when I feel cold and senseless like a dead clay, and surely you would be horrified by this if we embraced. (But is it true? How can he be writing all these things having spent the afternoon as he had, in a fever with Lucy? A fever heightened by the One he currently adores more than life itself, David Swancourt's Jello! Yet . . . does he adore Jello? No. That is not the word. What is the word?

Fascinated. Yes. This is better. He is, in a word, Fascinated. And the name of the galaxy he shares with her is: transgression. And a marriage, even with a woman like Akiko, always up for heat, for adventure, simply cannot provide what he craves. Yet the idea of losing her, another divorce, the horror of all this around him collapsing is frightful. Then again: what is the exact nature of 'this'? It eludes him. He looks at the trees, the books in their shelves, Kali so silent in her corner, and sees no meaning there.

Although . . . he has the good sense, after all—does he not?—to know, rationally, that it does somehow matter. Only—it has been shunted aside for so long it is almost impossible, it is impossible, for him to know why.

He writes:

For some reason, perhaps it will become clear to me as I write to you, Akiko, I recall being a small boy, my father having just punished me and leaving the room, locking the door behind him. I was in tremendous pain, an unnamable pain, that pulsed through my entire body, and yet I felt numb, immobilized. I thought: now I am like a soldier made of lead. I remembered the men my father once described, who died in trenches of clay only to become clay themselves over time. Something happened that day between my father and me that caused me to become like those fallen soldiers. I was in pain, but the heat of the pain was turning to numbness, the cold of the clay, and soon I lay in bed like a lump of clay.

But there is more. You must know that I have adored you. And we once shared an erotic heat, coupled with love, inseparable from love, and this is a thing I have never known before or since. I know you have longed to retrieve it, and this confuses me, or, rather, my response is more complex. I feel deeply sad about this loss of ours because I precipitated it. It seems I am incapable of sustaining any healthy impulse for very long. I hate the ease with which I lied to you as much as I hate your mistrust of me, your justifiable anger.

As a child I was plagued with guilt for the smallest infractions. I do not believe I was as bad as my parents thought. Only this: they were both in a rage against a world that was always off kilter.

And so my siblings and I matured in a house built upon a cesspool. Some sort of invisible slime covered everything, and this was incomprehensible to me. I imagined it was my fault. My parents both spent an inordinate amount of time in the bathroom. They could never be clean enough, nor could we. Our lives were ruled by black magic. What I mean to say is every aspect was ritualized, from the washing of sinks to the brushing of teeth.

My lovers are many things. They are bonfires within that bleak servitude, moments of heat and light. They are toys, they are archangels, they are demons. They are things to possess and to battle, to bring down. As were you, Akiko, they are hope. To annihilate.

When he is done, he pushes the page away with disgust and stands. He is feeling very strange. It is as if ice water is spilling on his head. Or in his skull. Yes: that is it, exactly. It feels as if his brain is bathed in ice water.

The letter pools darkly on the table like a malefic eye. It has a power, a terrible power all its own. He knows he must destroy it at once. He tears it into a thousand pieces before flushing it down the toilet. He thinks: *If the world is a dream, then fucking is as close to awakening as I can get. If the world is real, then fucking is as close to dreaming as I can be.*

A number of days will pass, a week. There is a silent understanding between them, a truce of a kind. They are temporarily giving one another time to think. Or, at least, this is how Akiko understands it. She knows that when they speak, it will be momentous, that nothing will ever be the same. Not only between them, but within herself.

She has moved into the studio and has abandoned the house, its kitchen, its theatrical elegance, its deceptive solidity.

14

LIKE A FERAL CREATURE fallen into a deep hole, Akiko paces. The studio, the house, the garden, the woods— even the air—all conspire against her. The world is leeched of luminosity and the clues accumulate. In a drawer she finds a book of names and numbers; she finds a handful of mysterious keys.

She broods over their second trip to Mexico. He had insisted upon a beach notorious for its danger. People drowned there every year, and the wife of a local doctor had broken her neck in the surf. He pretended to know nothing about it.

Her husband is not an emotional man. He is studiously calm. This calm of his is determined. Muscled, even.

She remembers how she watched him vanish each day. How, without a word, he plunged into the sea, pushing forward and riding the waves until he'd reached the outer banks of high water. This ferocity of his had impressed and silenced her. And she recalls his impatience when she had refused to follow him, voicing her fear of the severe riptide, the height of the walls of water; how a new fear she had refused to acknowledge (because it was a fear of him) had in that moment claimed her.

The acute strangeness of this memory is unfathomable.

And there is another:

One night, they had gone to a party at the Crucible. The beautiful boys in drag—chimeras he called them—circled him all evening. Had he given then appreciative glances, or had they been drawn to his frank virility, his vitality, his—could it be?—apparent susceptibility? Whatever it was, it was clear to everyone that in that hour, her husband was the prize they sought.

Not long after there was a patient, a new one, who seized his interest and whom he talked about over dinner. The patient, barrel-chested, hairy, showing up for therapy in a tight green leather skirt, high-heeled boots. She comes to think he had possibly told her everything but for the most important thing: their fucking. (This was back when she still blamed herself for her inability to understand, to appreciate the arcane process that went on behind closed doors. Day after day, week after week, year after year.)

She wonders if he fucks the city the way he had fucked the sea. She knows he does. A kind of horror overtakes her. It is a new feeling. She begins to entertain the possibility that her husband has brought her down in any number of uniquely imagined ways.

Akiko prepares herself for their encounter. She does not know, cannot know, that for him to be seen unmasked is an absolute impossibility. She does not know, cannot know, that in his solitude he has begun to somber in an ancient dream, a filthy dream, a prehistoric dream as old as he is himself.

Already the flies of death are buzzing inside his skull.

15

HE MOVES to the downtown cabinet. Three days a week he returns to Drear, ignoring the house, its garden, the park—to continue his work with clients. He has a new client in Drear, a man of middle age both unlike him and yet in whom he somehow sees himself: a man whose life is a failure. A man who has never married, who has always been a child, who has held on to his childhood fears, his longing for a vanished—volatilized!—mother, his life-long conviction that her vanishment was the result of an inherent flaw all his own, that he was both unable to keep her safe and unable to replace her loss for his father's sake. He describes the child he had been like a small circus animal unable to fulfill bewildering balancing acts for equally bewildering masters. As a child he was a weakling, preposterously insecure, and now he is still that way. He is also the Prince of the Non Sequitur, a Duke of Small Talk, the Earl of Platitudes. He is an eternal boy, an unhappy boy, dressed in a man's paper suit and as light as a feather fallen from the breast of a bird.

He is as thin as a wafer when he might have been *someone of substance, someone like the doctor; someone robust!*

But his doctor also wears a paper suit. In fact, he is rapidly failing. Since moving into Spells he is taken up with a terrible obsession—the snuff films he had begun to watch with the Cutter and cannot let go. Somehow he finds himself within them; he recognizes some truth about himself and the world that received him. In other words, their *weather* is familiar. It is the weather in which he spent his infancy and the weather in which his illness thrives.

At the same time he is attempting to extricate himself from both Lucy and the Cutter. Both of them clinging like glue. These days he is fighting to survive in an aquarium filled to the brim with glue. He wishes to be free of them both, to be alone with, seared and absolved by, the fever he shares with David Swancourt. Sex with Jello is rougher. He cannot, perhaps never will, get enough of her.

One night he and Jello are together in Spells, fucking like beasts on the floor. The Cutter shows up, maybe on a hunch, and finds the hall door open. The office is locked, but standing by the door, she can hear them and begins to scream. She demands he open the door. She demands he let her in. She says she knows he is fucking somebody. She says she thought she was the only client he had ever, would ever, fuck.

He and Jello fall apart and sit silenced, like scolded children, staring at the floor, waiting for it to stop, waiting for her to go. Finally she leaves, but first gives the office door a terrific volley of blows with her fists.

He sits naked and afraid, frozen in place and terribly ashamed. He thinks he must do the impossible: shed not only his skin, but acquire a new mind, a new brain entirely, a new heart. A new life! Or end this one, which might be easier. For the first time, David Swancourt sees just how vulnerable he is. Just how old. Until now he had thought of him as a "mature" man, a "mature, professional man." A "man to count on." But today Jello's lover has collapsed, is dwarfed by what is clearly a catastrophe. David stands and gathers Jello's clothes, her shoes, her hair, from the floor. With difficulty the Minotaur rises and ashamedly laughs; he says:

"I'm so sorry. I though I'd gotten rid of her."

"So, baby . . ." David Swancourt says slyly in Jello's voice, "I'm not the only fuckable client?"

"She," he says it slowly, as forcefully as he can, although he is shaking, "was the only other time. This," he makes a gesture of the hand, taking in the room as though it were the entire world, which in fact it is, "this . . . What happens here between us, is unique, unique in my life." He looks so tender, so worried, so forlorn, and suddenly somehow so trustworthy, that David relents, and Jello replies:

"I know it, baby."

———

Jello takes her time in the bathroom. She showers, applies her makeup, dresses slowly, pressing away creases with her hands. When she enters the street, she sees the Cutter, who has been waiting, perhaps for him, perhaps for them both. The Cutter sees right away what Jello is, and with an intake of breath, bites her lower lip. And Jello sees the glittering woman she wishes to be: her full breasts, her thin ankles and slender feet, her woman's throat, her pussy, the whole package. She is submerged in a sense of acute helplessness.

A cab approaches, and the Cutter flags it down. As David Swancourt watches her climb into the backseat, he understands that his lover, his doctor, needs his patients in the same way they need him. That the sex he exacts from them plays out the imperious need he has—for reasons beyond his own capacity to understand—for a sexuality driven by death.

David Swancourt hates his doctor for playing this deadly game of his. For fucking Jello rather than protecting her.

Jello returns to her little room in the Crucible where she looks at herself, undone as she is by the Cutter, and cries. David apologizes; he says:

"I should have kept you to myself. Why did I need to show you off to that fucker, who never replaced the blouse he tore from your body, did nothing but fuck you hard in the ass, no different from the other dicks in town—"

Jello replies. She says:

"Betrayal is the only thing you guys know."

David says:

"You're right. And now he's betrayed us both."

Jello disagrees:

"No. It's his fault. He is the doctor! He was supposed to protect the two of us. He was supposed to show you how to love me. But instead the two of you fucked me over. And maybe that's all I can hope for. Being fucked over and over."

Jello throws herself on the bed in agony. Her agony is his. In their agony they are perfectly joined. At last they fall asleep like Siamese twins, sharing a body, an agony, a heart.

16

THE WEATHER IS CHANGING; already the air is much colder. The Cutter is angry; she's devastated. Because she had prided herself in her uniqueness. The affair with her shrink had given her a powerful sense of her own specialness. A femininity so heady he had broken all his rules. How she had fawned upon him when she was not tormenting him! Each instant so precious because they had so little time. He said: We are the thieves of time. And this was true. The time he spent with her was stolen from his other patients, his wife. When they fucked the world was reborn. Their fucking was the one thing she trusted.

The Cutter directs the cab to the Chinese restaurant. As the city smears past, she thinks of his wife, so unexpectedly Japanese. Dressed, she thought, to kill. But Kat had seized the upper hand, if briefly, holding him in front of his wife, cutting her off, rubbing her out. Before he turned and walked away, his wife beside him, her own prettiness no longer easy to overlook. And she, the client, had gone off alone to her corner, their corner, while the shrink and his wife spoke together about the ineffable things that bind couples together despite all the odds.

And then she thinks of Jello again. The commotion they made in his office! Like a fucking battleground! She imagines walking into that office, at that very moment, and blowing herself up.

It's as if a thick wall of glass, an entire building of steel and glass, has shattered in her face.

The restaurant's familiarity is briefly a comfort. The waiter, solicitous; brings her a drink. In their booth she thinks: and yet. That innocence of his. The way he shuddered and cried out that first night when, as she nestled against him, the film, unabashedly evil, tore into the room.

The evening is early and the Cutter begins to drink. She remembers the first time she went into his office. The unmistakable light in his eyes that told her at once she had stumbled into a brand new possibility. She saw the way he played hot and cold with her depending on his fucking schedule. When he took her on Fridays the heat was constant, the day all her own. A sweet thievery, somehow immaculate.

There was a netsuke that fascinated her. She wanted him to let her have it. She needled after it: two wasps devouring the flesh of a fig. There they were, she said, the two of them, hungry and twinned.

The first time he saw her, she made sure he got a good look. She knew she looked her best in the late afternoon light. Amazing, really, in the bronzed light. Unprecedented. That was the word he had used. Deep in her cups, the Cutter recalls this. Ours, he had said, is an unprecedented adventure. What has transpired between us has never happened in all my years of practice, and it never will again.

"Stay with me just a little longer," she had wheedled, writhing against him.

"You . . ." he breathed it, "move just like a wounded snake."

The netsuke was called: The Wasp Carvers.

When she thinks of her shrink fucking a guy in drag, she can't stand it. The pain is so bad she'd do anything at all to rub it out. She thinks that maybe sometimes when his wife was away and he came to her in the middle of the night, he'd come directly from the Crucible. What if he'd been fucking guys all the while? How does she fit into that? And why did he bring his wife into their private place, this restaurant where they always went to be alone together when they wanted to talk? Be like real people. Suddenly the Cutter's stolen time with him is riddled with holes. So porous her life is leaking from the skin of her body. And because she is leaking, her thirst is boundless. As she drinks, the Cutter sees what he has hidden from her, all those people like herself, hungry for absolution. And he, the bastard, her shrink, the love of her life, the High Pope of tits and ass and cock and cunt! And they, all of them, wanting to be made over, penetrated to the marrow, rubbed into oblivion, yes: rubbed out. No: made visible.

Her shrink liked to fuck on bathroom sinks, on countertops, the floor. In the Studebaker. The Studebaker! She laughs out loud. She says out loud to no one in particular: "He liked to fuck in the Studebaker!"

In this way time passes. The Cutter loses her way. Around midnight she reaches into her purse. She always has a razor with her. An old-fashioned square Gillette, very sharp, with a good, solid top. She can get a good grip. She's in their booth, the one that is always empty and so always theirs. Once, early on in their *unprecedented* affair, he said: Eden is here.

If the Cutter is anything when she gets down to it, she is discreet.

She starts in.

She thinks if she cuts deep enough, he'll rescue her. Right now she's bleeding, she's crying silently in the night. She's thieving all the time she's got on her hands. It's a risky business.

17

When David awakens it is three in the morning. He decides to take action. He calls his doctor's office in order to leave a message. He is surprised when he picks up.

"David!" he says.

"Jello thinks you fucked her over."

He is frightened by this. He attempts to sound calm. In control.

"And you, David? What do you think?"

"I think you fucked her over. I think you fuck your patients over."

This makes him angry. Defensive. His voice rises. It seems to strangle in his throat.

"That's what you think! You think I fuck my patients!"

"I think you're as fucking scared as all the dickheads out there."

"Jesus—"

"I think Jello deserved better."

"I—"

"Don't say another word!"

"What can I do? What can I do to—"

David looks around his squalid chamber. He thinks of his doctor's office, its leather furniture, its gorgeous carpets and netsuke cabinet. He says:

"I think we could come to an agreement. Write me some postdated checks," she whispers. "O.K., baby? Hey! Write me a fucking book!"

───

He sits alone in his office, still as a spell, a stone, dead water. Finally he opens his desk drawer and takes a new checkbook out of its box. Just as he begins the phone rings. It is the hospital. An emergency. The patient is his.

───

When he sees the Cutter, he is undone. He is told she will survive the damage she has inflicted upon herself; that is to say she will not die, not yet, not this time. He sees to his horror that he has made his way into her body in unexpected ways, that his betrayal can be read like a road map across her wrists and thighs; she has cut the palm of her left hand, and there is a shallow mark, thin as a hair, but pearled with purple blood, across one cheek.

18

IT IS SUNDAY. He stands in the shower until the hot water fails him. He cannot shake the feeling that he is coated in slime. He goes to the sporting club and showers there; he takes a sauna and showers again. He returns to Spells and throws himself down on the floor, where he sleeps through the day and the night and awakens only at dawn when the sun tears into his eyes. It takes him a moment to realize it is Monday and that he must return to Drear to see a client.

The client asks him if he is unwell. "You are very perceptive," he says, "I seem to be fighting the flu." His tongue is swollen in his mouth or his teeth have grown uncannily large; it is very difficult for him to speak, his voice is not his own. His client says, you don't sound like yourself, and peers at him from behind his thick glasses with misgiving. He asks his client: "Would you like to end the session—you won't be charged—and come back next week? By then I should be over this." The client, who suffers paranoia, is very relieved and takes him up on this offer. The client, when he sees his wife later in the day, will say: "He looked so strange! I'm not even sure *it was him.* And I didn't like the way he smelled!" After a few hours reflection, he will decide to terminate his sessions.

That week he manages to see his clients on time, to get to both offices, Drear and the downtown Spells. He finds he has to remind himself, for some obscure reason, that he has two offices, has abandoned one; that Drear and Spells are offices, not "theaters." Except when he sleeps and they are both theaters in Hell where people are pleading and sobbing and damning him.

One morning, after an infinite number of mornings, he calls all his remaining clients to tell them he is ill and must cancel all sessions for an undetermined period. This surprises no one, because by now he is swimming in his clothes. Yet they are all profoundly upset and ask him whom they can see instead. But he had long ago broken from the psychoanalytic community in town, and has no idea whatsoever.

19

Akiko has finished her triptych and begins to prepare the entire show for the photographer and framer. For weeks she has been thinking about what she needs to say to him for weeks, what she needs to know. She calls him. She says, I am wanting to talk; I am ready to talk. She proposes they meet in town for dinner. She says: Vietnamese? Yes, he says. o.k. Vietnamese. And he offers to pick her up at home. She agrees. Off they go together in the Studebaker.

The Vietnamese is on a busy intersection, just off a major highway. Tonight the traffic is even heavier than usual, resolute, rageful. Death sings within his skull like a knife of ice within a tempest. When the light turns yellow he accelerates. When it turns red he tears into the unspooling highway, smack into the thick of it. When Akiko screams, her voice is as thin as any creature's struck down in the silence of the wood.

The author of eight novels as well as collections of short stories, essays, and poems, Rikki Ducornet has been a finalist for the National Book Critics Circle Award, honored twice by the Lannan Foundation, and the recipient of an Academy Award in Literature. Widely published abroad, Ducornet is also a painter who exhibits internationally. She lives in Port Townsend, Washington.

COLOPHON

Netsuke was designed at Coffee House Press, in the historic
Grain Belt Brewery's Bottling House near downtown Minneapolis.
The text is set in Spectrum.

FUNDER ACKNOWLEDGMENT

Coffee House Press is an independent nonprofit literary publisher. Our books are made possible through the generous support of grants and gifts from many foundations, corporate giving programs, state and federal support, and through donations from individuals who believe in the transformational power of literature. Coffee House Press receives major operating support from the Bush Foundation, the McKnight Foundation, from Target, and from the Minnesota State Arts Board, through an appropriation from the Minnesota State Legislature and from the National Endowment for the Arts. Coffee House also receives support from: three anonymous donors; Elmer L. and Eleanor J. Andersen Foundation; Allan Appel; Around Town Literary Media Guides; Patricia Beithon; Bill Berkson; the James L. and Nancy J. Bildner Foundation; the Patrick and Aimee Butler Family Foundation; the Buuck Family Foundation; Dorsey & Whitney, LLP; Fredrikson & Byron, P.A.; Sally French; Jennifer Haugh; Anselm Hollo and Jane Dalrymple-Hollo; Jeffrey Hom; Stephen and Isabel Keating; the Kenneth Koch Literary Estate; the Lenfestey Family Foundation; Ethan J. Litman; Mary McDermid; Sjur Midness and Briar Andresen; the Rehael Fund of the Minneapolis Foundation; Deborah Reynolds; Schwegman, Lundberg, Woessner, P.A.; John Sjoberg; David Smith; Mary Strand and Tom Fraser; Jeffrey Sugerman; Patricia Tilton; the Archie D. & Bertha H. Walker Foundation; Stu Wilson and Mel Barker; the Woessner Freeman Family Foundation in memory of David Hilton; and many other generous individual donors.

This activity is made possible in part by a grant from the Minnesota State Arts Board, through an appropriation by the Minnesota State Legislature and a grant from the National Endowment for the Arts.

To you and our many readers across the country,
we send our thanks for your continuing support.

Good books are brewing at coffeehousepress.org